TAKE THIS MAN
GAY ROMANCE STORIES

Edited by
Neil Plakcy

CLEiS
PRESS

Published in the United States by Cleis Press, an imprint of Start Midnight, LLC, 609 Greenwich Street, Sixth Floor, New York, New York 10014.

Printed in the United States.
Cover design: Scott Idleman/Blink
Cover photograph: iStockphoto.com
Text design: Frank Wiedemann

First Edition.
10 9 8 7 6 5 4 3 2 1

Trade paper ISBN: 978-1-62778-085-8
E-book ISBN: 978-1-62778-100-8

Contents

INTRODUCTION:
TO LOVE
AND HONOR

The iconic question "Do you take this man to be your lawfully wedded husband?" is engrained in the American psyche as one of the central parts of the wedding ceremony. Yet that phrase—and indeed that ceremony—could not be a part of the gay American dream until very recently. Now individual states have legalized same-sex commitments and marriages, and the U.S. Supreme Court has struck down the restrictive Defense of Marriage Act, and men all over the country—and indeed the world—are pledging to love and honor each other in the presence of family and friends, often with the blessings of civil and religious authorities.

Gay erotica, on the other hand, has always been about the thrill of first contact. Meeting, falling in lust and into bed (or whatever's handy). Exploring a new lover's body, learning what turns him on, feeling unfamiliar hands and lips on you.

How can these two traditions come together? This collection of erotic stories aims to answer that question.

How much sexier can an encounter be when the two men

involved have been together for long enough to make some sort of commitment—formal or not—to each other? When you know what turns your partner on, and vice versa, your encounters can be even hotter. When you are making love to a man, not just having sex. When your pleasure is so much deeper because you're with him, and you have a connection and a history together.

I hope you'll enjoy these stories!

Neil Plakcy
Hollywood, Florida

A GOOD HEART IS THIS DAY FOUND

Rhidian Brenig Jones

Eight hours after I'd fixed it in place, Iain bent his head to the rosebud in his lapel. "I can't believe he did this for us," he said. "I still can't believe he actually came."

"I knew he would, in the end. All the flowers are his way of saying he's okay with us now. You know my father, he'd never just come out and say it." I propped the bottle against my hip and turned it steadily, felt the cork give. "Pass me the glasses. Anyhow, all those posies, whatever they're called, that he made for the girls gave him a chance to show off."

He moved the curtain aside and looked down at the hotel lawn. "Party's still going strong. You're sure you didn't want to stay?"

"Nah, leave them to it."

"Reckon your mother's stopped crying yet?"

"Your mother-in-law, you mean? Not if she's still necking the gin."

The curtain swung back into place and he turned to me with

a slow grin. "My god, I've just realized. I've got a mother-in-law."

"So have I." I handed him a glass. "You know what she said when I was dancing with her? 'You're my second son, Christian.' Sweet. So here's to us, Mr. Leigh-Collier."

"Still think Collier-Leigh sounds better."

"I won the toss, darling, fair and square."

"So you did, so you did."

We clinked crystal and sipped, savoring the fresh, mineral edge of the Dom Perignon.

I asked, "D'you feel different?"

"Yeah, I think I do. It's as if…ah, I don't know how to describe it. It's as if a last piece is in place, everything's…complete." He took my hand and slowly rotated the slim platinum band on my finger, the twin of the one I'd given him. "I've said it a million times but I want to say it again, I want to say it now." He raised his face and looked solemnly into my eyes. "I love you, Chris. Whenever you think back to today, remember me telling you this. I love you and I always will."

Beautiful hands, my Iain has, strong and well shaped. The last hope for the gasping, blue-lipped babies who are brought to him. Precious hands. I lifted the left and kissed the ring, then pressed my mouth against his palm. "Remember that old Hollywood weepie, *How Green Was My Valley*, the one about the Welsh village? There's a cave-in at the mine."

"Kind of," he said, frowning, wondering where I was going with this.

"The blind boxer. The people try to talk him out of it but he's determined to go down the mine to rescue his friend. He says, 'He is the blood of my heart.' That's what you are to me, Iain. The blood of my heart."

"You've been practicing that." But he flushed with pleasure.

"I have. I wanted to say it right. Because I mean it."

His arms wrapped around me and I cupped his face as we kissed, gently at first, a soft brush to seal what we'd exchanged. But our mouths opened and he pushed against me and I braced my legs for him, my fists in his hair. We broke away to breathe and I kissed his neck and put my hand on his cock and it was full and hard for me.

"Bed," he murmured, arching his throat.

"Bath." I stepped back to look at him. Iain was tall, too slender, maybe, but it meant that clothes hung beautifully on him; he'd look good in a Mother Goose costume. The restrained formality of the traditional black morning coat somehow emphasized his masculinity, the absolute maleness of him, and it occurred to me that it might be an idea to skip the long soak I'd planned. "You look as sexy as hell in this."

"I'll fuck you with it on if you like."

My cock cramped, and for a second I wavered. Forget the bath. Just shove my trousers down and bend over the bed. No foreplay, just get him in me. A wipe of lube, that slight resistance and the long slide in. But I shook my head: your wedding night, you don't have a quickie. And I've always enjoyed the torture of anticipation, of spinning things out.

He rolled his eyes. "You and your bloody baths. Well, you get the tap end."

"They're in the middle but it doesn't matter. I want you to lie on me, lie on your back so I can see your cock."

He raised an amused eyebrow. "Sounds like a plan."

"Why do they float?" I asked.

"Ask Alastair next time we see him."

Iain's friend, a consultant urologist. A gay consultant urologist. I reached for the soap and peeled off the wrapper. "I don't care what you say, cocks up to his elbows, it's bound to turn him on."

He gave an exasperated sigh. "Christ, how many times have we been through this? It doesn't work like that."

"How d'you know? He could be as hard as fuck under his scrubs."

"I *know*. Christian. Hearts are my job, cocks are his. Surgeons don't get turned on by the job, especially when half the time it's fixing eighty-year-old dribbles. Geologists don't get turned on by rocks and shales and, and...sediments, do they?"

"Course we don't," I said loftily, lathering the hair on his chest. I dabbed some on his nose. "But a nice-looking little geode, all sparkly, winking at me...well, that's a different matter."

"Idiot." He sucked a shivery breath through his teeth as I ran my nails over his midriff and his toes bent reflexively. "Oh, yeah...and here."

"The guy I love: part man, part gibbon." I dug into his armpits, worked the silky fans of hair. Iain loves me to straddle his ass and scratch his back. He hugs the pillow, burying his face and grunting softly as I hash his skin with livid tracks. There's nothing sexual about it; he just likes the sensation. More often than not, especially when he's wiped out from work, it sends him to sleep. But sometimes I'll spread my hands to caress, and my cock gets hard as I sense his response to the change. Down I go, skimming my palms over his sides, the dark puff of hair at the base of his spine, to his buttocks. Kiss him there.

He said, "There's something poking my ass and it's not soap. It always turns you on, doesn't it, the thought of Al and all his cocks? It's why you keep on about it. Perv."

I flipped water to wash away the foam. "You turn me on."

"Do I? What is it about me that turns you on?"

The way your semen pumps over the back of my hand when

I jerk you off. Your tongue delving into my slit. The sounds you make when you feel me coming in your ass. "Your navel. Nice little outie button."

"My navel."

"Yup."

"Your ears do it for me."

"Do they? Hmm. Not much point going to bed if it's going to be all about ears and navels," I said.

"Suppose not...oh, might as well. The water's getting cold. We can tuck up nice and warm. I've got a couple of papers in my bag about atrial fibrillation in children. I'll read them to you if you like."

I'd been keeping my eyes off his cock, the delayed gratification thing again, but finally I let myself look. It lay on his belly, fully erect, as rigid now as mine. I swirled a soapy fingertip around the gorgeous circumcised head. "Or we can make love."

He covered my hand and pressed. "Or we can make love."

One long leg dropped to the side, he lay on the bed in an elegant sprawl. The light from a single bedside lamp gleamed on the curve of his shoulder, the sweep of his rib cage. His muscled flank led the eye to his thigh, lean, dusted with dark hair. My gaze traveled back to the center of him and I watched the glints dance from his ring as he stroked idly, keeping himself at the simmering point.

"What?" he asked with a lazy smile.

"Just you."

"Like what you see?"

I unwound the towel from my waist. "What d'you think?"

We don't have to ask or explain, not anymore. A look, a gesture, sometimes not even that, is all it takes. So when he raised his eyes from my cock and slid his heels to his ass, I knew the way it would play out. But I said it anyway because I wanted to try the words for the first time. "You want your husband to fuck you, baby?" A tremor passed over his face and his cock clenched, lifting off his belly. The bottle of lube had rolled next to his hip and he felt around for it. I stroked his instep. "Not yet."

"Don't make me wait, Christian."

"Just a little while."

I have forty pounds on Iain, hard-packed muscle, the result of lucky genes, my place in a rugby front row and the occasional resented hour in the gym. So when I crawled up between his legs I hovered over him, straight-armed. He ran his hands over my shoulders and biceps as if he'd never felt them before and his need for me throbbed in the blood vessels at his throat.

"Safe. I'm safe with you."

"Always." I lowered my hips and fitted my cock to his and in the last second before I kissed him, very low, almost under his breath, he whispered, "Beloved." The thought came to me then with eerie clarity, fully formed. *Whatever strength is in me, whatever power I have, it's for you. I will guard you and protect you. I would kill for you.*

"Let me," he murmured, breaking away with a gasp.

"Let you?"

"Suck."

I hesitated. Once his mouth was on me, the way I was feeling I wouldn't be able to hold back and this night of all nights I needed to be inside him. "Don't make me come."

"I won't."

Up, then, on one elbow, he flattened his palm on my breast-bone. "I love your tits. I love it that you're smooth."

"Thought it was my ears."

"Those too."

Lapping like a cat, he worked back and forth, breathing on the moisture trail he made, rubbing the ball of his thumb, gently flicking my nipples. Iain's aren't sensitive but when he settled to suckle mine, each rhythmic tug of his lips sent a hot flare to the mesh of nerves in my cock. Groaning at the sensation, I spread my legs. The first time he'd taken me to bed, he'd hurt me. Just that once, never since. A couple of months earlier he'd ended a going-nowhere relationship with another doctor—hot sex, tepid emotion—and he'd misjudged things with me. Maybe lust had made the deft surgeon clumsy for once or maybe he'd simply been used to a guy who was into rough handling. Whatever the reason, he'd tugged too hard and the gray bolt of pain that had shot through my balls made me nauseous. I'd curled away from him, tucking into myself, hardly able to hear his stammering apologies. We all get it wrong sometimes and I'd already fallen heavily for him, so I stuck with it. It had taken some time and more than one heated conversation before I got to the point where the approach of his hand didn't make me flinch. But that was then.

His forearm brushed my shaft as he reached down and found that sweet spot behind my sac, pressing just firmly enough so he didn't tickle. His hand cupping, fingers lightly drumming, he manipulated my balls the way only he can, watching my face, the quivering of my cock. But when he lowered his head and mouthed my glans, I clutched his hip. *"Don't make me come, Iain."*

"Sure?" He held my shaft at the base and painted the tip wetly over his lips. "You're sure?" A swift duck of his head and I was engulfed in heat, the bed of his tongue soft, the roof of his mouth hard. Up in a spiraling suck. Down. Up, the maddening drag of his lips. Down. Up, a sly little finger stretching to my hole—

I pushed at his forehead and eased out, my heart hammering. I sank back on the pillows and dropped my arm over my eyes as I fought back the rise. "Fuck." He started to kiss up the side of my shaft. "*Don't!*" I let out a shaky breath. "Don't. Christ."

He reached down over the side of the bed and picked up the towel. "Do it then. Now, Chris. I mean it. Now."

That moment. The man you adore on his back, his hands clasped behind his knees, holding them to his shoulders. His cock engorged, southpaw balls drawn up high at its base. Naked in its ruff of fur, his anus cramps with desire, the sweet pink corona pouting. He's fractionally dilated and you press a fingertip against the rim to get a glimpse of glistening, rose-red membrane. He smiles at you, he's waiting for you, and the world is reduced to your own aching cock and this little pursed mouth and your man's hoarse pleading.

Mouth to mouth…I kissed him hungrily, my lips soft but the scrape of my stubbled jaw harsh on his perineum and the under curve of his sac. I nuzzled into him, rasping delicate flesh. He'd be sore in the morning, the way he likes. I held his balls away and slid my tongue into him, easy, easy through the relaxed muscle. Only with him: Iain is clean and wholesome and whatever we do together is an expression of love.

It takes time to learn a man's body, to move with him far beyond the default jerk and suck that'll get anyone off. Iain likes to fuck me belly down, claiming it's so he can rock on the cushion of my ass rather than grind his bony pelvis against bone, but I think it's more my submissiveness in that position that excites him. As it does me. But this night I wanted him on his back. I wanted to kiss the taste and smell of his ass onto his face. I wanted to look at him when his orgasm hit. I squirted a coil of gel and began to massage his perineum, up toward his cock, following the thick ridge as it bisected his sac. His balls separated, hanging on either side, dense and heavy. I swept my hand from the root of his shaft to a slithering stop just short of his hole and with the other I grasped him, pulling it gently upward, feeling the responsive ripple as I squeezed and released, squeezed and released.

"Oh, fuck..."

My mouth was bone dry. I cleared my throat, swallowed hard. "What, babe?"

"You know."

"No, I don't. Tell me."

His head rolled on the pillow, tossing in frustration. He knew I'd make him say it. "Inside me. Finger me."

"Like this?" Just a fingertip at first, teasing dips hardly penetrating the supple ring. "Or this?" All the way in until my palm was splayed against his buttocks and I heard his sharp, gasping cries. His rectum sucked at me, slippery with lube and his own sweet fluid; I could feel a pulse, the frantic beat of his heart. And there...I swept my finger over the plump bulb, caressing, caressing, and watched his cock grow limp: when I do this to him, the sensations in his ass are so overwhelming, he occasionally loses his erection. Sometimes I can make him come, soft as he is, with just my fingers. I looked up along the length of his body, from the wiry bush at his groin to his lovely face, dark eyes heavy lidded, his mouth slack. There was no love in the look we exchanged; there was only the hard light of lust, the primal glare of two men in rut.

My hands shook as I coated my shaft. Again I hovered, but this time braced on one arm, my other hand guiding my glans to his hole. Finding the angle for entry...under and up, following the slope of the bowel, high in, high in, oh Jesus, so high into him until I hit the cage of his pelvis, the barrier that keeps me out. Keeps me from entering fully into him, merging his body with mine. He held the back of my neck and his legs locked around my hips. His mouth was against my ear, murmuring, urging. My face hidden in his neck, I began to thrust. Unable to think, unable to feel anything but the heat and the wet and the staggering pleasure in my cock. The glory of fucking him.

"Bite," he panted.

It's a hangover from his adolescence. Iain's first boyfriend used to mark him all over with love bites and he still likes having it done to him. I bit at the join of his throat and shoulder, sucked a sliver of skin hard against my teeth. He bucked violently and I felt the almost overwhelming urge to sink my teeth into the muscle, bite it hard, a male animal pinning its mate. My heart galloping, I leaned my brow against his. Storm clouds of orgasm were gathering, piling in the distance; already I was feeling the first warning flickers, the flashes of lightning in my cock. *Focus. Focus on him.*

"Again, bite me some more—"

"No!" I gathered him to me and surged into him, jolting his body with each savage thrust, lost to everything but the need to come, to empty my seed into him, flood him, fuck him, *fuck him—*

"Yeah, baby, *yesss...*"

I half-heard his crooning moan but then there was nothing, nothing more of him or of me. I lifted into the vortex, my climax spinning me, spinning me, and I convulsed into ecstasy and I broke apart.

Sated and dreamy, I cuddled into him, drifting comfortably down into sleep. He moved slightly and I hooked my leg over his thigh and pressed a kiss onto his chest. It was wet with sweat and smelled of sex. I caressed his belly; it was damp too, slightly sticky. Sleepiness evaporating in a sudden cold rush, I swam back to the surface. *Damp.* No slippery wash of semen. My eyes snapped open. "Iain?"

"Mmm?"

"You didn't come."

His arm tightened around my shoulder. "I didn't, love, no."

"But..." I sat up. "Why not? What's the matter?" I yanked the sheet away and stared in disbelief at his erect cock, the glans shiny, straining against its frenulum. "*Iain?*"

"Come here." He pulled me down and kissed the top of my head. "I stopped myself coming."

"But why? How the hell did you stop yourself coming?"

"After the pounding you gave me, you mean?"

"Well..."

"I can do it when I want to. Chris, listen. We got married but a marriage has to be consummated, doesn't it?"

"Does it?"

"Yeah, I think it does. The way I see it, two men, well...how would it work for two men?" Under my cheekbone, his heart had taken on a rapid, thumping beat. After a moment, he said quietly, "They both fuck. They fuck each other."

I smiled as I finally understood. "Yes."

He rolled onto me and kissed me savagely, grinding my lips against my teeth. "Where's the lube?"

"I don't know, it's here somewhere..."

"Better find it quick-smart, babe, because your husband is going to fuck you." He reached his hand over my hip to my ass. "Fuck you forever."

INTO THE DARK

D. K. Jernigan

This was the worst fucking idea, *ever*." My headlamp illuminated Rick from behind, and I glared daggers at his back; not that he was paying any attention. Ahead of him, his own light only seemed to cut a small slice from the oppressive dark that closed in around us. "Cave hiking sucks. I want to go back."

"I told you, I've done this before. Don't be such a baby."

So much for our big, romantic day off. With our demanding schedules, it was hard for Rick and me to coordinate time off together, and *this* was how we were spending the day? "We're lost."

"We're not lost. I swear, I know where we are. Do you want me to show you on the map, again?"

"No, what I *want* is to go back!" We'd been walking through darkness for about an hour, the only illumination coming from the lamps mounted on our hard hats. Outside, it was a good ninety degrees, but in here the temperature plummeted, and I was already wearing the heavy coat Rick had insisted I bring.

And "hike" was a bit of a misnomer, too. Sure, there was hiking. There was also scrambling over rocks, crouching in low passages and climbing up short rock walls. It was dark, it was scary and I was on the verge of seriously freaking out.

Ahead of me, Rick sighed. I could see the tension in his shoulders and took it as yet another sign that we were lost. And doomed. I kicked a small rock on the ground, and Rick winced as the *crack* of its impact with the wall echoed around us. He turned, carefully keeping the headlamp pointed down and away from my face, and I glared straight at him.

"This was stupid. We're never going to get out of here."

"No," he said, with exaggerated patience. "We're fine. We're almost there. If you don't like what I want to show you, we can go back. Okay?"

"Why can't we just go back now?" I asked. Sure, I sounded petulant, but I was cold and tired and not a little freaked out. The cave felt like it was closing in on me, and the darkness was choking and stifling. I shuddered as I turned my head, trying to illuminate more of the cave, but the darkness swooping in behind the beam of light only made me feel worse. When I turned forward again, I saw that Rick had already started out ahead of me. I hurried to catch up, and resumed glaring at that tense spot between his shoulders, right above his backpack.

"Trust me, it'll be worth it," he said, as if he could feel my eyes on him. He passed around a rock column in the middle of the cave, and I followed, dragging my feet. At the end of the passage, the rock walls seemed to squeeze together, forming a narrow opening.

"No way. I'm sick of squeezing through little holes."

"Turn your light off."

"What? No! No fucking way. I want to go *back*."

Rick turned and took my hands, and I narrowed my eyes at

him, trying to resist being charmed or sweet-talked. It didn't really work. "Mason, I need you to trust me, okay? What I want to show you is just on the other side of that hole. Please? For me?"

He'd been walking backward, pulling me toward the opening with each step, and I sighed dramatically as we reached it, and reached up to switch off the lamp. I could feel my face drain of blood as our light was cut in half, and Rick's face was plunged into darkness. My heartbeat sped up and I started to tremble. This was the stuff of nightmares, buried beneath the earth under tons of rock, alone in the dark.

Or almost alone. Rick gave my hand a reassuring squeeze and turned off his own lamp, and I whimpered involuntarily as we were enfolded in the darkness. He pulled me gently forward, and I felt for the opening with my free hand, ducking to squeeze through the tight passage. Two steps, then the walls expanded and I could stand straight again. Not so bad, except for the dark.

And then Rick dropped my hand. I yelped in shock, but he murmured soothingly from just ahead of me. My fingers itched toward my headlamp, and I started a slow count to ten in my head. He had ten seconds, and then I was giving up on this bullshit and turning my light back on. Ten seconds... God, it felt like forever!

I was at eight, and panting, when I saw a glow kindle to life ahead of me, then grow brighter. I looked away from Rick and his lantern (where had he gotten a lantern?) to keep from hurting my eyes, and what I saw made me gasp with wonder.

The entire cavern glittered and shone with crystals embedded in the walls. It was like a fairy wonderland or some magical palace, hidden here in the ground where only the dedi-cated—or those with romantic and determined lovers—would find it. A fitting reward for over an hour of fear and frustration in the dark, despite the fact that I hadn't done much to earn it.

I stepped forward and put a hand to the wall, feeling the cool smoothness of the crystal embedded in the rock. It was so marvelous, it took me a moment to realize that Rick had been standing next to more than a lantern. I turned slowly and faced the scene, and felt instantly like a total prick.

He must have come down here on his day off, yesterday, and gotten things set up for us. There was an inflatable mattress, fully inflated, and a bottle of wine, well cooled in the chilly air. He went down on one knee as I turned to face him, and my heart about stopped.

"Oh, Rick..."

"Mason. Will you?" He held up a ring box with a solid gold band, and I felt tears gather.

"Are you sure you still want to after all my whining?"

He grinned. "As long as I have permission to tell everyone that you whined and bitched the entire way to the proposal."

I held up my hand for him, and he slid the ring onto my finger; a promise made and sealed in gold. "Deal. You get wineglasses down here, too?"

"I wanted to, but it seemed like a bad idea. We've got plastic cups. You game?"

"Definitely." He poured, while I emptied my own backpack of food. I had wondered why he had insisted on me bringing impractical treats, like a box of strawberries. And why I'd had to carry all of it.

But when he sat on the mattress opposite me, and I took the first crisp, sweet sip of wine, food was the farthest thing from my mind.

"Thank you for dragging my lame ass down this hole," I

said. He took it for the apology it was, and leaned into me, and our lips met in a searing kiss that made the hairs on the back of my neck—and other things—stand up. I wished I could bottle the feeling and pull it out whenever I needed a pick-me-up, because there is nothing more energizing than feeling exactly how loved you are.

His kiss told me all that and more, and soon we were lying back on the inflated mattress, doing a whole lot more than kissing. His hand brushed the stubble of my cheek, teasing my sensitive skin and sending shivers of excitement through my entire body. I took my own explorations to his waist, where I knew he was not quite ticklish in a way that made him incredibly horny. We teased and played, our tongues sliding over each other and our hands wandering.

Then Rick grabbed my cock, and I knew that it was time for much, much more. I took the cue and kicked free of my pants and shoes, and he sat up to pull his shirt off at the same time. I chuckled when we came together again, each of us half-clothed, and pressed our lips together hard in a kiss that was as much a battle for dominance as it was a gesture of love. Seeing as I had been a dick all day, I fought back only long enough to make Rick feel good about winning, then let him roll me over.

He bit at my shoulder blades as I got onto my hands and knees, wobbling on the squishy surface of the bed. "Hurry," I whispered, and the cave brought the echoes of my plea back to us.

"I am," he assured me, and the slap he delivered to my ass echoed as well, though it didn't cover the sound of his pants being pulled down, or the condom wrapper tearing a moment later. Then I heard the little click of the lube bottle, and a second later he was pressing against me, his cock hot and hard at my opening. "You sure you want this?" he teased.

"Come on, Rick, fuck me." I pressed back into him, but he shifted, forcing me to wait.

"I don't know, maybe we should eat first. It was such a *long, exhausting* hike." I could hear him trying to suppress the laughter in his voice, and I rolled my eyes and moaned, begging him without words.

This time he did laugh. But he followed it up with the ultimate reward, thrusting into me in one smooth motion. My body opened to him, and I moaned in pleasure as I adjusted to his girth and the glorious sensation of being filled and possessed by the man I loved.

"God, move!"

"God now, am I?" He wiggled his hips just enough to drive me half out of my mind, then began to pound me in a slow, steady rhythm that I knew he could hold all night long. I gasped and clenched around him, desperate for more and wanting more than anything to entice him into losing control. He slapped my ass for my efforts, and apparently decided it was fun. I groaned when his hand descended again, and then a third time. The stinging swats only made me hungrier.

I started to reach for my own swollen cock, but Rick batted my hand away and bent over me. When his hand closed around me, the pleasure immediately began to mount. He stroked me in time to his own steady thrusts, but my heavy breathing and whimpers of pleasure were starting to get to him. When I cried out at an especially pleasurable stroke of thumb over crown, he gasped and his pace became faster and more ragged. I pushed back against him, begging him with my body to take me to the edge.

"I love you like this," he whispered, and then he granted my wish. He slammed into me, plunging me deeper into the pool of pleasure. His balls slapped against my ass as he fucked me fast and hard, our animal sounds of pleasure magnified and returned to us by the chamber walls until we were surrounded in a cocoon of eroticism. I tried to hold back, but his skilled hand on my cock was persuasive, and I shuddered with sensation as he made me come. He continued to stroke me, his hand lubricated with my fluids, and I moaned and trembled in sensory overload.

"Fuck...yes. Damn, Mason." He sounded like he was speaking through gritted teeth, and I bore down around him one last time, ready to pull him over the edge with me. He came with a roar that echoed deafeningly around us, and drove himself deep into me.

He pulled away a few seconds later, and we collapsed side by side on the narrow mattress, clinging to each other for warmth as much as anything else. "Still think this was a bad idea?" he asked.

I chuckled. "Maybe not the worst, but don't expect me to help you pack all of this shit out of here."

I could have smacked him when he answered, "My backpack is empty. Why do you think I made you carry all the food?"

MY APOLOGIES, SIR

Kiwi Roxanne Dunn

The door closes behind them with a quiet *click,* but the gentility of the sound doesn't belie Luther's anger. Luther Aristotle Philadelphus (yes, that's really his name) is always controlled, even when he's furious. Owen Sean Monahan watches the slight tremble in Luther's fingers as he hangs his plush, green-tweed coat up on the lone peg by the front door. That tiny shiver is the only visible indication of the anger that Owen *knows* is simmering beneath the surface of Luther's placid calm. The only indication of it that Owen is likely to get for—well, however long Luther decides to keep him in suspense. *Ah, the privileges of command,* Owen thinks. *To be able to pull rank.*

He feels a hot flush of shame stain his cheeks at the thought. That's not fair, and Owen knows it. First Lieutenant Luther "Iceman" Philadelphus, until only recently affiliated with the USMC, to which Owen still swears allegiance to this day, has never been one to cling too tightly to his rank.

When Luther first arrived to take charge of the battalion, the bunch of angry, disenchanted Marines would have cheerfully ripped him to shreds the first week if it hadn't been for Owen fending them off. It was Owen who had quietly ass-reamed the men (and women, as there were a few of them, too) into giving Little Lord Fauntleroy a chance.

Luther had won the men over with his blue eyes and pitch-perfect leadership skills. He had succeeded brilliantly in his role as commanding officer, though the whole battalion knew Luther was gay. Not that it mattered; the era of DADT was blessedly over, so everyone could go back to the normal, everyday business of trying to figure out who was shagging who. But what stood between Luther and Owen was rank. Officer and enlisted were the real taboo now. They were like oil and water; fire-breathing dragon meets dust bunnies; that sort of thing.

Luther had a broad muscled back, working-class physique and truly enormous size-sixteen feet, which had always seemed tailor-made for combat boots. He seemed to have come out of the womb six feet tall and Nordic. Born with an M-16 in his steady hands. Even those ice-blue eyes seemed designed for tracking prey.

Owen should have known this was a bad idea: flying halfway around the world from England to turn up at the doorstep of Luther's tiny student-housing Harvard apartment without so much as an invitation. He should have assumed that the shock of his presence—unannounced and unexpected—on Christmas Eve, might not be anything his ex-CO would want.

But then, it had seemed too good an opportunity to pass up—after months of emails and passive-aggressive 2:00 a.m. IMs and the innuendo-laced Skype calls, in which Owen tried vainly to shock Luther awake for his 8:00 a.m. class while Luther spluttered and blushed over his second cup of black Starbucks

Espresso Roast—to see him in person. *What a wonderful world it would be,* Owen thinks, grimly, without the slightest attempt at Christmas cheer coloring his thoughts. *More fool me.*

Owen still wasn't sure if their covert-ops affair had been the deciding factor in Luther's decision not to reenlist after his initial service was up. Perhaps he should have asked. But it was a little late for that now. Luther was a *mister,* not a *sir,* and in his second year at Harvard Law School, so the whole question was (or is) now most decidedly a moot point, as Owen uses the moment it takes Luther to unwind the white, doughy scarf from around his tall and shapely neck to wonder why he'd even assumed Luther would be alone for the holidays.

Still, Owen can't help but remember the mingled shock and anger he'd felt, ringing Luther's doorbell not six hours ago. He'd been greeted, not with the reserved happiness he might have expected from his former LT, but by a decidedly tipsy and unusually boisterous Luther, shrouded in a halo of Christmas-tree lights spilling out from inside and surrounded by half-a-dozen of his grad-school friends. They'd all been on their way to a Christmas party on the other side of town, and Owen had been left stammering his apologies to Luther's white, wide-eyed expression.

Owen's hands clench tight against his sides. Now is not the time to push Luther's buttons, and Owen knows it. He can see it in the hard, thin press of Luther's posh, plump lips, the angry furrow of worry lines in his forehead. But the silence is getting to Owen, eating at him, and all the knowledge in the world can't seem stop a soft "Sir—" from slipping past Owen's lips.

The word is barely more than a breath, a quick exhalation of air that leaves Owen's lungs like a punch. It still ought to be enough to provoke some sort of response from Luther, but the silence only lengthens. When Luther's still quiet, even as he kicks off his loafers and pushes past Owen into the apartment, Owen's hands start to sweat. But he's here now. And he's not going to run away from this. From Luther.

"Sir—" But when Owen tries again, his voice is rough. It hurts to swallow, and there's a dangerous heat building behind his eyes. "*Luther!*" Owen breathes, as he moves to follow Luther into the privacy of his living room. If it sounds like begging, Owen doesn't care. Much. He has to believe that this is salvageable. That his presence hasn't ruined whatever tenuous connection they'd managed to keep alive between Luther's studies and Owen's stint with the Royal Marines.

"Look at me!" Owen growls. This time, he punctuates his words with a grab at the sleeve of Luther's corduroy vest. The fabric feels strange—wrong, even—in his hands. For the first time in his life, Owen longs for the familiar discomfort of their MOPP suits. He needs something to ground him. Some sort of sensory data that he can lock on to, and catalog—that will once again mold Luther into any one of a thousand easy definitions: *Sir, CO, Lieutenant Philadelphus.* But when Owen tries to pull Luther in for a soft kiss—to apologize, in the only way he knows how to—Luther ducks.

"Not *now*, Owen!" Luther barks, and his tone is the same one he used to shout down another CO the first time Luther refused to get them all killed: curt, polite, but with a dangerous edge lingering underneath. Maybe that had been the moment he'd won them over: by saving all their lives without even realizing he was doing it. But Owen's nothing if not daring, and if Luther is what winds up killing him, not some bullet or stray shrapnel shard, so fucking be it.

"Yes, *now!*" Owen tightens his grip on Luther's sleeve, and twists the cloth hard between his fingers before adding, "*Sir.*"

Luther's face, as he turns to face him, is white with anger, but his voice is all pained surprise as he says "Owen. What—?"

Owen doesn't so much answer Luther as slam him up against the wall, hard enough to make Luther's teeth rattle. Luther makes a noise, on impact—a soft grunt of surprise. Owen has just enough time to see Luther's eyes go wide, and watch him struggle to draw a breath before he crushes his mouth to Luther's and kisses him like it's the last chance he'll ever get. Owen feels Luther push against his chest. There's something nearly frantic about the gesture.

Owen wonders, briefly, if his shove knocked the wind out of Luther, and promptly realizes he doesn't care. This gesture—message—*whatever,* is more important. Owen lets his tongue twine around Luther's. He sucks on it until Luther shudders against him. Then Owen draws back just enough to nip savagely at Luther's bottom lip. Luther groans, and Owen tastes blood before he moves to soothe the wounds with his lips and tongue. By the time he finally pulls away again, Luther won't shut up.

"Owen—Owen—" Luther pants. His hands claw for purchase in Owen's too-short hair, and he squirms until one of Owen's legs is sandwiched between both his thighs. *"Owen!"*

"Sir," Owen mutters back. His voice sounds oddly broken, but Luther doesn't seem to notice. Not that that should surprise Owen, what with Luther pressed up against him, and already hard. Achingly so, Owen would guess, if the way Luther's practically sobbing his name is any indication.

This isn't exactly how Owen envisioned his apology going. He'd pictured more talking, less fucking. Maybe a few angry condemnations on Luther's part. For a second, Owen is tempted to slow things down, to get to the part where they talk, and yell, and ask questions. But then Luther cries, "Jesus *fuck,* Owen!" positively pleading now. So Owen just slips a soothing hand between Luther's denim-clad thighs. He rocks his hand, and his palm slides hot and fast over Luther's rock-hard cock.

Owen means to say that he doesn't belong in Luther's world, that he'll leave in the morning. Really, he does, but what comes out instead is a choked *"I'm sorry. I'm sorry, sir. So fucking sorry!"* as he fumbles with Luther's fly.

"Fuck, Owen!" is all Luther says. Luther's voice is thready, but there's a dismissive quality to his words that Owen doesn't understand.

"Sir?" Owen asks, but Luther's only answer is a quick, hard bite at Owen's ear that sends tingles all the way down his spine.

"Bed," Luther orders. Owen would ask which way, but Luther disentangles his legs from where they're wrapped around Owen's waist, and slides down the slope of Owen's thigh until his stocking feet brush the floor.

"Bed," Luther commands again, a wicked grin ghosting across his lips as he hooks his hands in Owen's shirt and pushes him toward the hall. Owen catches a flash of tinsel from the corner of his eye as Luther manhandles him down the narrow corridor. Owen wonders how he missed the enormous bulk of the Christmas tree in Luther's living room the first time around. He can only conclude that Luther's presence fucks with his situational awareness. Owen opens his mouth to tell Luther this, and wonder aloud about the kind of person Luther would bother to decorate a tree for, but Luther kisses him quiet. Kisses him until Owen's giddy with it, and he lands (with a soft *oof* of surprise) on Luther's mattress.

Owen hadn't even noticed turning the corner into Luther's bedroom, and he thinks about that as the bed dips beside him with Luther's weight. Then, Luther's hands are trembling over the zipper of Owen's jeans, and Owen pretty much loses track of conscious thought for a while.

When Owen comes to, Luther's on his hands and knees below him. Owen's buried deep inside Luther, and splayed across him, so that his chest is pressed flush against Luther's back. Owen presses his cheek against the sweat-streaked hollow between Luther's shoulder blades and breathes, shallowly, in and out. Luther gasps below him. Luther's quieter than any of Owen's other lovers ever were. It used to worry Owen, before he'd come to understand that Luther would always be subdued about his feelings, even in bed. Luther doesn't talk, or scream. A quick moan here, or a muffled curse there, is about as vocal as he'll ever get. Owen's learned not to expect Luther to tell him what he likes and doesn't like.

Owen figures it out in other ways. He knows Luther's in ecstasy when this one muscle in his lower back twitches, just *so,* beneath Owen's hands. He can trace Luther's pleasure along the hard, bunched line of muscle down his forearm. When Luther fists the covers, twisting the sheets between his fingers until his knuckles go white, it means he's happy.

Owen cups Luther's fist with his own large hand, so he can trace the peaks and valleys of Luther's knuckles. Luther shudders and opens his fist just enough for Owen to slide his hand in. When Owen does, Luther sighs. He twists his grip until his slippery fingers slide between Owen's.

The steady panting of their combined breath is loud in Owen's ears as he stares at the sight of their hands, locked together, against the bright white of the sheets. On another night, a different night, Owen would worry about how unavoidably *gay* that image is, but since he's pretty sure that this is the last time he'll ever get to do this, it seems okay. Owen clutches Luther's hand tight in his, and thrusts in time to the tempo of Luther's breath, driving Luther—driving them both—ever closer to the edge. Owen loses himself in the rhythm, in the steady back-and-forth of their bodies, and does his best not to think about the morning.

Owen wakes at sunrise, just as the first streaks of light stain the slate-gray sky outside a faint, rose-quartz pink. Luther's still asleep, wrapped up in the blankets like the Christmas— Hanukkah—present that he isn't, and Owen knows it's time to leave. He has to go before Luther wakes up and tries to stop him. If Luther wakes up, and Owen's still here, he'll feel compelled to do the right, polite thing and talk Owen out of it, even though Owen's presence is the last thing Luther wants in his life. Luther proved that much last night.

It takes Owen only a few minutes to dress. He's big, and broad, and burly. He doesn't need a lot of time to look good. His freckled face, coal-black hair and gunmetal gray eyes do the job credibly. Owen doesn't even reach for a change of clothes this morning, just slips on the same black jeans, wife-beater (the better to show off his beefcake arms, all tatted up), and motor-cycle jacket he'd worn the night before. His bag is by the door, fully packed.

Owen stands to leave, pausing only to think back to the disaster of the party the night before. He'd insisted Luther go, had tried to tell him he'd book himself a hotel room and be gone in the morning. Owen recalls the way Luther had fought with him about it, made a scene in front of his friends and finally (after Owen had refused to let him back out of his prearranged plans) dragged Owen to the party with him. The hours there had been awkward and strained. Luther had been tense and irritable the entire time, and refused to socialize with anyone. He'd spent the evening in a secluded corner with Owen, glowering, white-faced and silent, as he'd resolutely ignored the profusion of both presents and alcohol that swirled around them.

Owen tiptoes through the living room as quietly as he can in size-twelve combat boots and tries to summon up a righteous surge of anger at the memories. He's surprised, instead, by how much he really wants to stay. Luther still feels like home to Owen, even after he's clearly moved on to other people and a better life.

Owen's so distracted by his thoughts that he almost doesn't see the flickering glow of candlelight, until it's too late. He only *just* catches the quick flash of it, from the corner of his eye. Owen turns, right hand firmly clutching the shoulder strap of his duffel bag, and stares at the menorah sitting in Luther's living room window. Owen looks at it for a long moment, wondering what it means, before he shakes his head sharply, slings his duffel bag over one shoulder and turns to open Luther's front door.

"Owen?"

Owen doesn't mean to freeze at the sound of Luther's voice. Doesn't mean to stand there, rooted to the floor, as the syllables of his name spill like drops of molten silver from Luther's tongue. Owen tells his feet to move. He screams the order silently within the private walls of his own, thick skull, but they won't budge. Owen swallows. He can't seem to run, so Owen does the only thing he can: he closes his eyes and counts out every jarring, frantic beat of his heart against his ribs.

"Owen—" When Luther finally breaks the silence, Owen allows himself a moment to drink in the perfection of the sound. His name, on Luther's lips, is a thing of beauty, and Owen wonders how he never noticed it before. "Owen," Luther says again, like it's the only word he knows. Luther sounds sleepy, sated and almost drunk. The barest prickle of curiosity colors his words like the slight tingle of spiced rum.

"Sir," Owen answers. His mouth is dry. Turning to face Luther feels like work, but Owen does it anyway, and gasps—

audibly—at the sight before him. Luther's stark naked where he stands in the middle of his living room, shrouded by the soft glow of the early morning sun. Tongues of crimson fire lick his skin. The color brings out the russet in Luther's hair, and stains his cheeks a faint, dusty pink. Luther looks—he looks arresting. Angelic. For a second, time stands still.

Then doubt flickers across Luther's face and he steps forward, out of the sunlight. The spell is broken, the aura gone, and Owen is plunged back into the icy grip of his own fear as he waits for Luther to figure out what's going on.

"Owen—what?"

Luther steps a shade closer to Owen, hesitating over the movement, like he's not sure whether it's allowed. Owen watches something like fear flit across Luther's face. It's with shock that Owen realizes Luther's—*uncertain,* in a way he never was in Iraq. Owen feels thrown. He's not sure how to handle this and he knows he's not trained for it. Owen is the one who's supposed to have the answers.

Owen's never seen Luther look so lost before, and part of him aches to course correct, to soothe away the worry he sees etching lines on to Luther's face. "What are you doing?" Luther asks. He says the words slowly, like he hasn't fully processed what he's seen, or maybe he hasn't woken up.

His eyes skitter across Owen's fully clothed form and land on the duffel bag clutched tight in Owen's hands. "You're— you're leaving?" Luther is all bewildered accusation even as he steps clear into Owen's space, pressing up against him until their noses nearly touch. And something about the combination of that tone and gesture cuts Owen to the quick in a way that no strangled shout, or barked order, ever could. Fleetingly, Owen wonders what he looks like. Wonders what emotions are playing out across his face as Luther presses a gentle palm against Owen's cheek. Luther's fingers are rough, lightly calloused from typing, and Owen leans into the touch although he doesn't mean to.

"Sir—" he says, just as Luther chokes *"Don't."* Owen licks his lips, waiting for the tirade that he knows is coming, but Luther's eyes widen a little and he waits for Owen to speak.

"Please—" It isn't what Owen means to say at all. Owen's not sure why he feels the need to apologize for anything. He's doing this for *Luther's* benefit, after all. This is—this is what Luther wants.

"Please what, Owen?" Luther's voice is like a touch, featherlight against Owen's lips. And Owen tries to answer Luther, but he finds he doesn't quite know how. He winds up stammering, blinded by the ice-blue brilliance of Luther's eyes, and the sudden graze of Luther's thumb against his bottom lip. "I—I—I—" Too late, Owen realizes he's trembling. He wants to look away, but Luther won't let him.

Luther's fingers lightly stroke Owen's temple as he crowds even closer. Owen has the wild thought that they made love just last night, but this moment feels more intimate than fucking ever could, and then Luther's kissing him. Luther kisses Owen's tremor away, and only pulls away once Owen's wrested back his trademark calm.

"Talk to me," Luther pleads, before adding, *"Stay!"* Owen flinches at the sound of Luther's voice—raw, and little used. Under any other circumstances, Owen would consider it his duty to soothe away that tone, in whatever way he could, but he can't, now. Not when he's the one who put it there in the first place. Owen makes himself step back, and thinks that that one, small action—stepping away, from Luther, might be the single hardest thing he's ever had to do. When Owen speaks, though, his voice is steady.

"I don't belong in your world, sir," Owen says, and something dangerous flares in Luther's eyes, at that.

"You do if I want you to," Luther says, with a stubborn tilt to his jaw.

Owen snorts, harsh and grating.

"Yeah," he answers. *"Right."* It's possibly the most disrespectful tone Owen's ever used on Luther, and Luther looks lost again, but this time, the expression angers Owen more than it moves him.

"Want me?" Owen asks, and it's him that crowds into Luther's space this time. The movement is defiant and unapologetically threatening. Luther looks startled. "You didn't *want* me last night, sir."

"Of *course* I wanted you!" Luther says, and he looks like Owen struck him, but Owen doesn't care. Not now.

"You've got a funny way of showing it," Owen spits, and he might almost feel bad about it if it weren't for the fact that nobody can move him the way Luther Philadelphus can. Nobody else can make Owen feel this—vulnerable, this exposed. Owen realizes that he's let his guard down around Luther, in a way that he hasn't around anybody since his ex. He knows, from all those months of fighting with him, how important the next few seconds are. How critical it is to hang on to the upper hand while he still has it.

"What was that at the party, *sir?*" Owen asks, and he can't help but enjoy it, just a little, when Luther flinches at the emphasis on his rank. "I told you that you could go. And then what do you up and do, but drag me along, and act like your night is about as much fun as pulling teeth? I mean, what the *hell*, sir? You barely talked—barely *looked* at me, the entire time. You didn't—you didn't introduce me to your grad-school friends. Fuck, you didn't say so much as a single word to anyone. So don't stand here and tell me that you *want* me. That I belong in your world. Not after you made it abundantly clear last night how much I *don't!*"

"Jesus Christ, Owen!" Luther shouts back. Luther's gone nearly white with rage, or something else. He's naked and gorgeous and everything that Owen wants and won't ever be allowed to have. "That wasn't about *you!*" Owen makes a sound at that, and finally whirls around, his hand on the door he should have escaped through ages ago. Luther's talking rapidly behind him. Owen doesn't want to listen, but he does.

"You never gave me a chance *not* to go, Owen! Did you ever think about that? You show up on my doorstep, and then assume that I—that I—" Luther sounds winded, like he's grasping at straws. "I see those people every week, Owen! Why the fuck would I want to go their party when I could spend time with you?"

Luther lapses into silence. He slumps near the door frame, and Owen realizes with a jolt that Luther *does* want him, but he's also not going to stop Owen from leaving. Not if that's what Owen wants.

"You—but—you were pissed that I was there!" Owen finishes, lamely.

"Owen—" Luther says. He sounds like Owen's words hurt him, and Owen feels something twist in his gut at the expression on Luther's face. It's open, and honest, and almost as vulnerable as Owen feels. "I'll never be pissed off because you're here." Luther's voice is so low that Owen can barely hear him.

Then Luther steps forward until both his palms are pressed against Owen's chest. "I didn't want to go to that party." Luther speaks slowly, carefully, like he's terrified Owen might misinterpret his words somehow. Owen's not entirely sure Luther's wrong about that. "Not after I saw you." Luther swallows, and

looks away. "I—Jesus, Owen, I hoped you'd come. Dreamed—"
Luther makes a face. "Why *else* would I put a menorah in the
windowsill, Owen?"

Owen stares. His heart is beating rapidly in his chest and he
has a feeling Luther can hear it. What's strange is how little he
seems to care.

"The menorah's for me," Owen says. It's not a question, but
Luther answers him anyway.

"Duh," he says, with an exaggerated roll of his eyes. Then
Luther reaches up and flicks Owen's nose, lightly, with his
thumb. If it were anybody else, that would piss Owen off.
Instead, he tilts his head, leaning in toward Luther until they're
almost within kissing distance.

"And the tree?" Owen asks. His breath tickles Luther's
eyelashes and he watches as Luther closes his eyes and breathes
in, deep.

"Lot of trouble to go to if there's not gonna be anybody else
around to enjoy it."

"You waited," Owen says, bewildered. "You—why didn't
you tell me?"

"Why didn't you?" Luther counters.

"Point, sir." Owen reaches for Luther's chin with one hand
and wonders what it says about him that he's still surprised when
Luther doesn't pull away. Luther makes this noise when Owen
kisses him, soft and needy, and Owen lingers over the kiss for
far longer than he intends to. Owen kisses Luther until Luther
moans, long and deep. Then (and only then) Owen pulls away.

"I—I didn't get you anything," he says. Owen's chest is
heaving and it hurts to breathe, but it's okay, because Luther's
gazing up at him with wide, lust-blown eyes, and he looks—he
looks *in love.* The realization makes Owen's words stutter and
die in his throat.

"Owen." Luther's smiling, but Owen could swear he sees a slight sheen of moisture in Luther's eyes through the mingled glow of the candlelight, and the rising sun that's slowly turning from red to gold on the horizon. Luther looks amazed, like he can't quite believe what he's about to do. Then, he leans forward, standing on his tiptoes to reach Owen's ear. "All I want for Christmas," Luther whispers, so soft that Owen can barely hear him, "is you."

STRANGERS FOR THE NIGHT

T. R. Verten

H e awakes with a start—the daily jolt of *shit, dinnertime, shit, bath time, shit, bedtime, shit, parenting*—but no, they've gone to their grandmother's, where they will stay for the whole weekend—oh, wonderful, *glorious*, sweet relief—and so flops back down into the pillow to snatch back the quickly unraveling threads of his dreams. An hour or so later, the rumble in his stomach stirs him a second time; he stretches unhurriedly. As he rubs the tendons of his neck, he gropes his way into the hallway, eyes cloudy with grit. He trips over Michaela's elaborate Lego castle and knocks over a turret in progress, one of the yellow pieces embedding itself in his bare foot.

The inside of the fridge makes him regret skipping the weekly Trader Joe's run for sleep. The doors are stocked with low-acid orange juice, Horizon 2%, San Pellegrino, and Reisling Kabinett. The shelves hold cartons of yogurts, unfinished fruit and vegetable purees, prewashed carrot sticks. There is turkey, at least, and the end of a loaf.

He clears away the medical journals cluttering the kitchen table to eat his sandwiches. The bread is too dry, he decides, should have toasted it first. He eats, though, and exchanges texts with Cathy. Yes, she confirms, the kids are fine. Guilt pangs Shawn's stomach, and he refills the water glass with cold white from the fridge.

He can't always be there, and hell, he may be a parent, but he has needs, too. That's what tonight is for, for him, for the itch he has to scratch. It's early yet. The club scene now comes alive after eleven, crowded with guys from beyond the city limits. Those who will come from the far stretches of the South Side, like he used to, a route he could probably still navigate through a drunken stupor: Jackson local to the green line, an outdoor transfer to the red, back down below the belly of the city, a walk up piss-scented stairs to surface at the lights of the city center.

He could end up at a place with flashing lights and pulsing bass; he can play at being nineteen again. But early, this early on, he opts for a shower. Shawn makes it a scalding hot one because he's got it all to himself, unlike yesterday morning, and plans his outfit under the steam. A fitted shirt, he decides, to show off his arms. Soapy water sluices down his back and legs. Before he shuts off the taps, he rinses his balls with a cupped hand, and then drips his way into the bedroom. Button-down shirt—without the possibility of spit-up he can wear white, plus it sets off his skin, jeans—no, too casual—trousers are better, a soft charcoal twill. He slides black boxer-briefs up over his narrow hips, puts the rest on. Wallet, keys, phone now dim with no one to text.

He walks five blocks to the red line and sits under a broken heat lamp. The 9:47 train's delayed by ten minutes, and when it rattles in, his car turns out to be packed with shouting teen-agers. Shawn pretends to study the ads for dentists and community colleges while they whoop and shout, hanging off their seats, passing a crumpled water bottle filled with the product of creative siphoning from parental liquor cabinets. They leave, thankfully, at Belmont, leaving him with late-shift hospitality workers and drunks who'll ride the line to the end. The air outside isn't much of an improvement from that underground, but he catches a whiff of the thawing lake, the burned smell of tar and stone coughed up by the afternoon's construction projects. The potholes of winter are being filled in, orange cones directing traffic into one light-clogged lane.

"Evening, sir," the doorman nods, as he enters the lobby. Shawn tilts his chin in acknowledgment as he unwraps his scarf, shoving it in his pocket. He glides past the foyer, with low-slung seating, artfully arranged single orchids, small groups of women stirring swizzle sticks. Beyond another door dim yellow lights and the seductive clink of glassware beckon. He scans the room, seeing straight couples canoodling in booths. Not the kind of place he'd have picked. The drinks list is printed on translucent rice paper. Shawn has experienced this before, at an outlandishly spendy seventh-anniversary dinner at Alinea. Served with a flourish, the waiter murmured in reverent tones that the menu itself was their amuse-bouche. He shudders at the memory.

"Can I explain the cocktail menu?" a bright-eyed mixologist asks.

"No," he tells her, as he rubs it between his fingers, swallowing away the remembered taste of glue, "I'd rather you didn't." Her eyes narrow, trying to suss him out—hammered, asshole, business traveler, shitty tipper, what? He orders a Crown and Sprite. The first sip jolts his tongue awake, the next spreads warmth down his neck.

"Are you staying at the hotel?" she asks each customer who

bellies up to the bar, and he, in turn, flicks his gaze to them, so as to establish his presence without overt interest—a man in dark purple cashmere, who's working on a laptop and orders a 312, a cute blond glued to a cell phone, who covers the mouthpiece to order vodka, two twentysomethings in sloppy business casual, pastel shirts untucked, who order rum and diet soda and bleat their evening plans to all who will listen. The bartender shares his smile of relief when they're poured into a taxi by the doorman, away to terrorize the town's improvisers at the second set.

"Another?" she asks, indicating the empty glass. Shawn nods his assent. She sweeps away the crumpled napkin and salted pistachio shells. He drums his fingers on the bar, keeping tempo with her as she pours, shakes, strains and places a fresh drink before him. He pulls out his phone, resigned to wait as long as it takes. Which, as luck would have it, lasts for only two games of Tetris and a scroll through Twitter. Nothing from Cathy, but he keeps the ringer switched on, just in case.

"Are you staying at the hotel?"

"Yes," says a crisp voice, "Room 502."

"I'll charge it?"

"Thank you."

Shawn's attention snaps into place. He looks up from the political bickering of his timeline with relief; here he is, the one he's been waiting for. That melodious voice belongs to a man of middling height and dark red hair, whose average features cohere like a discordant symphony. Shawn's fingers clench the slippery stem of his martini glass. *Tanqueray and tonic*—he hears him order—*lemon, please, not lime.*

Shawn drinks him in: his sinful mouth, curved around the lip of his glass, the teasing flick of his pink tongue, as he licks the gin from his upper lip; his slow-spreading smile to the bartender as she hands him his own tiny silver dish of pistachios. He catches Shawn's eye and holds the stare that beat too long, then walks his drink and his dirty, angelic, dick-sucking face over to a corner table. His tight shirt was a bad idea, he thinks, since sweat is suddenly gathering in his armpits.

Shawn undoes the top two buttons of his shirt, twisting as he does so to watch him walk away, but the seat lies just beyond his range of motion. The windows, fortunately, reflect the man back at him, and he takes full advantage, tracking the quick motions of his hands as he cracks open the nuts, the delicate purse of his lips as he licks salt from his fingers.

He tips, then, with his ass falling off the leather, a graceless flail of limbs and momentary loss of his center, before he grabs the edge of the counter and rights himself. Shawn sits very still and wills himself to look at the counter, the bottles, the bartender, but he can't help it, he's too adorable, his mouth is obscene, he would destroy it given half a fucking chance… his breaths come quick and shallow, the drive to look already turning his head once more—

—and Tanqueray has sidled his way over, seeping his way into Shawn's orbit. Their shoulders brush, electric.

"You look like you could use a drink." The ice clinks as he fishes out the wedge of lemon and brings it to his lips. Sweat drips down his own glass, which has managed to empty itself once more. The room tilts a fraction and his cheeks grow hot. He could use that mouth on his balls, to start. He could use every piece of this guy, fill every hole he has and then some. Hell, he almost says so. Jesus, he's old, if two drinks can send him sideways. Shawn blinks, yellow spots pop up behind his eyes. His throat is thick and dry.

"Maybe," he manages. "I'm getting there. She," Shawn nods at the bartender, "pours a good cocktail." Not his best line, but better than sitting there stupid and silent. Those red lips split into a naughty smile. "I'll have to catch up to you, then—" He signals her for one more.

"Same again?" she asks Shawn.

"Could you get us a bottle of Pellegrino? One more of these," the redhead says, ice rattling in his empty glass, "and that's on me." He turns to Shawn, "I've got a table." *Yes,* Shawn tries to say, *I saw you come in. I was watching. You're beautiful. I'd very much like to fuck you.* What comes out: a garbled: "Yes, I can see that. There you are."

"You get the glasses." He picks up his fresh drink and the green bottle; Shawn follows, watching his ass bounce gently in crisply pressed gray dress slacks. The pants follow the curves in the front as well, clinging to lightly muscled thighs and up the inseam...he can almost taste the wool, how it would fuzz up his tongue and suck the moisture from his mouth. Swallowing, he finds he still has spit. Tanqueray breaks the seal on the water and pours.

"These are new trousers," he tells Shawn. The bubbles tickle his nose. "I've been out shopping today."

"You're visiting?" Shawn asks, dumbly. God, he's *awful* at this.

"Mm. Ducked out of my conference and went to Saks. It's naughty, I know."

"Oh?" For eleven years he's been out of practice with pickups, the flirting and innuendo, but he clears his throat nonetheless. "They're very nice, it's—erm, shit—you look nice."

"Nice?" He tuts into his drink. "Not quite the reaction I was hoping for when I bought them, but I'll take what's on offer."

Shawn can do this, he's danced these steps before. All he has to do is remember how. "I mean, the pants are—good. They look tailored. Expensive?"

Oh, that's totally the wrong thing to say, they've only just met, they're strangers, they don't share a bank account and fight over money, but the other man smiles all the same.

"Very," he replies, mouth curving upward. He then lobs another question over, his a smooth backhand in contrast to Shawn's own clumsy, unpracticed strokes. "Do they suit me, do you think?"

A hint of a smile plays around his lips. Surely he can see how Shawn's affected by him, drawn like metal to a magnet. Do they, *fuck*. His voice prickles the back of Shawn's neck. When he speaks again, his own voice wells up thick in his throat, alien to his own ears.

"I'd have to take a closer look," he says, "to be absolutely sure." Gaining confidence from the other man's rising blush, he continues, making the words gravelly and intimate. "I didn't see much, but those pants, however much they may have cost"—the stranger's eyebrows go up at the mention of money—"they are worth every single cent."

"Yes," the man breathes out with a happy sigh, "I was hoping you'd think so."

Glass emptied, Shawn reaches across the table to touch him, rubbing tiny circles into his wrist with his thumb. The stranger bites his lower lip, and Shawn wants to take it between his own teeth to taste the blood and feel the sting. The man clears his throat and says, "I saw you looking, before. When you were sitting alone. At the bar."

His heartbeat flutters beneath Shawn's touch, thready and quick. "And?" Shawn bends his head to press his mouth against his pulse point. Words, he can't master, but the touch is doing the trick.

His lips part, "And I think you need to go get your credit card back," he answers, "because I'm holding you to that promise."

"You said you've got a room?" the point of Shawn's tongue flicks out, cleaning away the salt on his skin.

"Upstairs," he says, eyes half-shut in drowsy pleasure; it's late for them both. "Do you want to come see it?" As if this hotel could be all that different from any other, with its luggage racks and industrial towels, miniature bottles of booze and shampoo, cheaply framed art depicting local scenery.

"If you'll let me," he says, teeth grazing the fleshy meat of his thumb. The other man stands quickly on shaky legs. Shawn's face is nearly level with his groin, and the pants are so tight, the outline of his cock is already noticeable. He looks around, checking that they won't be seen, and then cups the other man's crotch appreciatively.

"I really want to see what's underneath"—he tugs on the pants leg—"these." With one finger he traces the stiffening curve of his cock, a soft swell in the fine, silky fabric. Shawn is fairly sure he's not wearing any underwear, and he licks his lips, meaningfully, trailing his fingers down the other man's quadricep. The muscle twitches there, too, the nerves electric. His thighs are wonderfully sensitive, even with the barrier of cloth between probing hand and bare skin. Shawn wants to seal his mouth over the bulge and lick the expensive wool until it's sodden with his own spit.

"We don't have to go upstairs," he says softly, making every word count. "I could take you in my mouth right here, right now." The man flushes even more deeply, his breath coming fast and ragged, face twisted up with shameful pleasure. He delivers his words to the expensive gray fabric, whose exorbitant cost is now forgiven because of the way it so beautifully gives away every twitch and flex of the hard cock beneath. He continues, "You'd like that, wouldn't you? For everyone to see how you are, all these people watching you come apart, watching me suck your cock?"

The tug on his hand yanks him up from the booth, and Shawn chuckles as the man walks to the doorway sideways and stiff-legged, hiding his hard-on behind a hibiscus topiary, as he signs the tab and avoids the curious gaze of the bartender. Then together they begin the long journey from bar to lobby to bedroom.

"You fucker," the man says, once they are alone in the elevator, with only the security guards watching on their basement monitor, "you absolute fucking bas—" Shawn swallows the words, and the kiss floods his mouth with the herbal tang of gin, and the sweetness of his mewl, the slam of his hand atop the stranger's, pinning him to the wall. "Tsk," he says, at the swearing. "You want me to put my cock in you?" Shawn asks, cupping his buttocks with his free hand. The man wriggles in his grasp.

Already he is panting, a flush painting his cheeks, his mouth red and kiss-swollen. Shawn, tongue loosened with alcohol and want, is suddenly on a roll with the dirty talk; the guy fucking loves it, so he continues, "You like that? The idea of me fucking you"—for a moment he hesitates, since they haven't exchanged names, have simply been thrown by chance into the delirious momentum of an anonymous hotel fuck, but he has to call him something, right, something besides *Lips* or *Pants* or *Tanqueray*, so he tacks on—"baby?"

"God, yes." He shudders when Shawn's teeth catch his earlobe. "Want it, all of it, all of *you*."

"Course you do," he growls as he palms that perfect ass, hitching the man's leg around him. The movement draws the new pants tight around slimly muscled thighs. His own cock clamors for more attention, but his hands are busy grabbing fistfuls of tight ass. With their tongues pressed together, Shawn grinds his hips down at the same time.

The door pings on the fifth floor, sliding open with a swish. They tumble forward into the hallway. Ten paces past the foyer he sweeps the stranger up in a wet, filthy kiss. He wriggles away and veers left. "This way," he says, blue eyes gone dark.

Shawn walks stiff-legged himself now, as he trails his prey down the still corridors. His lips seek the stranger's once more as they sneak past the ice machine. He stands a head shorter than Shawn, and when they kiss, he lifts onto his toes, the better to fit their mouths together. His mouth trails below his jaw, a slick motion that earns a heated gasp. God, the *sounds* he makes when Shawn pulls on his hair, red silky strands that slip between his fingers.

"Has it been that long?" he whispers to the sensitive spot that sits right behind his ear, "because you're practically begging me to fuck you here in the hallway." Shawn seals the indecent words with a lick from ear to neck, as the green light flashes, and together they stumble forward into the room.

"I've been—ah—busy. With work and—things. Oh, oh, shit that's good." Shawn chuckles to himself: who's doing the swearing now? With one hand, he tugs open the man's belt buckle, unbuttons, unzips: the silky trousers slither to the floor; the other hand steers their mouths together, the shorter man straining around to reach Shawn's lips. Commando, he realizes, as his hand grazes bare skin, just as he'd thought down in the bar. Shawn brushes his fingers across the man's belly. At the touch, the stranger lets out a strangled cry. "Oh, god, Sh—"

Shawn grabs his jaw once more, catching him in a rough kiss before he can get out the words, swallowing his moan. "Shh," he says, smoothing a hand down the front of his body, "not now, baby, not when you're being so good. You want to be good for me, right?"

He opens the blue shirt, hands dipping down between each

button so he can stroke that lovely cock, tugging on it from root to tip, an overhand pull, one hand after the other. Up and down, avoiding the glans, tugging down on his balls to keep him grounded. He needs that small bite of pain in everything they do, be it the yank on his hair, or the smack of his ass, or the twisting bite of teeth on his inner thighs while he's getting fingered. It doesn't make him any less impatient, though, for even now he's mumbling, pleading. "Fuck, need you, need you in me, please. Please."

He swallows hard. Lord, but the begging gets him low in his gut, loud and twisting like crumpled cellophane, every fucking time. "Go get on the bed." The pants tangle and slow him down, but Shawn still manages to lag a step behind. He pauses to take in the perfect composition of his partner's body, how his shirttails frame his dimpled ass. He lies down with his feet propped on the floor, tracking Shawn's movements as he pulls open the bedside drawer, looking for lube. A copy of the yellow pages; eyeglass case; a heavy gold wedding ring, engraved with two pairs of initials; a black plastic prostate stimulator and a matching rubber cock ring; a plastic bottle, newly opened, barely used. He picks the last of these.

The man watches quietly as Shawn slicks his fingers. His hands unfurl and close in anticipation, picking a rhythm out from the folded edge of the sheets. The movement reminds Shawn of a kitten, tentatively feeling out its first steps beyond the whelping box. He sinks to his knees in front of the open drawer and presses a kiss to the inside of his left knee, lifting the foot to place it on his thigh. White teeth grind against his full bottom lip, swollen from Shawn's stubble. A flick of tongue to soothe away the burn.

Face gone flaming, he rolls his hip open so Shawn can see him, pink and perfect. One finger surges forward, for Shawn finds hardly any resistance there. "Oh," the man sighs. Inside, too, he is slick and stretched, quick to take a second finger. "Yes," he breathes. "So good."

Open, Shawn can feel, and his own cock surges to think of him here, late afternoon light picking out the muscles of his arms and the rucked-up sheets as he fingered himself, surrounded by the mess of shopping bags and the casual disarray of a space not his own. He would have been on his back, legs spread, slim fingers slick with lubricant as he made himself ready to take Shawn's cock.

"You did this," he breathes, the realization hitting him low in his gut, the heat of his lover spreading down Shawn's whole arm, suffusing him with warmth. "Here, on this bed, getting yourself all ready for me."

The man's pale chest heaves in time with his frantic nods, "Y-yes," he utters, and looks down the length of his body— naked and exposed from the waist down, precome smearing his smooth stomach, mixing with sweat, staining the hem of his shirt, Shawn crouched between his open thighs like a pred-ator—and as one they watch his ass clench, then yield, as Shawn adds a third finger, slowly thrusting them in and out. "I wanted to be ready—oh fuck—right there, Jesus, sh- shit—you, fuck..." His head falls back against the pillow.

"What did you think about," Shawn asks, "when you did it?" He swallows. "A strange man filling you up, splitting you open?" Without removing his fingers, Shawn comes to stand, towering over his partner. "You," the redhead gasps, a sound made all the sweeter by the knowledge that it is Shawn, only Shawn, who can do this to him. Strands of hair cling to his forehead, a blotchy flush dots his cheeks. They share the air as Shawn leans in and closes the distance between them. The words are full of love and pleasure so thick it fills the room.

"Take my cock out, baby," he murmurs, the dirty words filled with tenderness. He reaches up through his spread legs to fumble at Shawn's fly. The pink tip of his tongue presses against his teeth, his brow contracts. Concentrating. Metal clanks as the buttons open and the zipper is yanked down. Both hands grasp for Shawn's erect cock, the trailing brush of fingers and caress of cool air.

The stranger's mouth spills open when Shawn pulls his fingers out; a filthy wet sound fills the silence. With a soft gasp the man watches wide-eyed, staring down past his stomach. Shawn positions himself, slings one leg over his shoulder, as the man underneath him groans. He doesn't bother to reach for more lube, since they're both soaked through, but swipes the fat head of his cock along the man's crack, gathering the excess, then lines himself up. He cradles the back of the man's head with his hand, forcing his gaze down to watch.

"Look," Shawn breathes. "Look at yourself, picking up strangers, so desperate for it. Look at how I'm going to fuck you, baby, look." The fistful of hair he's grabbed is sweaty, but it doesn't matter, Shawn's got him pinned, pretty well bent in half, perfectly ready to split open.

The words come out as a moan, "Yes, yes, fuck me, please," the man whimpers. Together they watch the tip of Shawn's cock as it disappears, the gleam of the wet shaft sliding into the darkness of their conjoined bodies.

The man clenches and fucking wriggles on Shawn's dick. He mouths his shoulder, scraping teeth along the muscle. "You feel even bigger than you look." "Christ," Shawn groans, stilling his hips. He settles in deep until he's fully sheathed. The other man's cock twitches, red and heavy against his belly. The stranger clenches around him, and then releases, tilting his hips so Shawn can fuck in deeper. Through his nose, he takes a deep breath, willing himself not to shoot off right away. The other man, though, his partner, does not like that decision one bit. He wriggles, again.

"No," he pleads. "Don't stop. Fuck me harder," he insists, ass clenching, and Shawn bites off a curse and starts to move. Sliding out, and coming home, so tight every time. He pounds him into the mattress, because they cannot hold back the tide. Tomorrow, he decides, rocking into the narrow cradle of the other man's hips, tomorrow I'll eat him to delirium, wake him with my mouth on his balls and a finger up his ass, and in between we'll call for room service, for mediocre hamburgers gussied up with aioli, French fries that will be cold before they even arrive, losing their crisp heat on the ride up five floors, but it won't matter one bit, lazy and sated, wild-haired and fucked-out, he'll eat them anyway.

"Yes," his lover moans, as Shawn fucks him, "there, Shawn, Shawn, oh—god, please let me let me." His cock is gleaming, twitching each time Shawn slams into him, nailing his prostate on every thrust.

"Do it," Shawn commands, to the humid curve of his husband's pale throat, "come for Shawn, come for me, baby." Their hands intertwine, and Shawn shoves down his hand, pinning his partner as he comes undone, spasming and moaning so loudly, like they can't at home, never alone, and fucking out all those little sighs and groans makes him drive into Brian all the harder.

He awakes with a start, as he does every morning. The kids are with Cathy, and he has overslept. The sun streams in at an angle too high for early morning. It is quarter till ten, Shawn sees, when he looks at the clock, and Brian—hair mussed from sleep, swaddled in a white terry-cloth bathrobe and wheeling in a cart that promises to contain French roast and multiple varieties of melon—smiles fondly down at his husband.

"It's late," he gripes, accepting the china cup from his position on the bed.

"Mm," Brian hums, sipping his own coffee. "Someone needed sleep."

Shawn scrubs a hand over his face and takes another sip of coffee. Brian cracks his fingers. Shawn, as he does every morning, winces from the sound. Brian tips his head from side to side, stretching his neck, and in doing so, exposes the pale line of it to Shawn's hungry gaze. There are bruises purpling there, faint teeth marks scored against the skin, which Brian absently traces a finger over.

"Look at what you've done to me," he purrs.

Shawn swallows, heavily, the unspoken suggestion to Face-Time the kids and Brian's mom now stuck in his throat. Brian catches the furrow of his brow, reads there the anxiety of the full-time dad and gently he detaches the coffee cup from Shawn's hand and places it on the end table.

"It's their naptime," Brian says, unknotting his bathrobe. A pale sliver of skin reveals itself as the fabric parts. "We don't want to wake them up," he adds. "We'll call after." *After,* his eyes sparkle, *after you fuck me into the mattress again.* Already, he feels a stirring, a need to glut himself on Brian, to mold his body to his own and feel him anew. Today, and every day from now until they die.

"After," Shawn agrees, reaching for the man he loves, "they'll be much happier after their nap."

"Quite right," Brian agrees, and leans in to kiss him.

TABLE
FOR THREE

Jameson Dash

B ette had her laptop open and paperwork spread across the bar when Toby arrived at the restaurant. "You're late," she said. She gave him a look over her reading glasses.

"I thought you worked better without me over your shoulder."

She shrugged. Then she said, "The new kid starts tonight." Bette pushed her glasses up into her braids. She reached out and patted his hand when Toby groaned. "You hired him," she said.

He did, but Toby forgot he was starting tonight. He wanted him in the restaurant as soon as possible, to get him training. Instead of throwing the kid in the deep end of weekend service, they were starting tonight, a Wednesday. It would be a nice, slow night to ease the kid into the job so they didn't lose another server in another month.

They had lost three to grad school in the last year, and the latest position had already been filled twice. Toby was hoping this kid would stick around.

"Tell me his name again."

"Mike."

Toby groaned. "Why would I hire a Mike?" He wandered into the kitchen, Bette's laughter fading into the sounds of cooks and cooking. He stopped to chat with Mo, who was working out the night's menu on the back of the day's receipts.

"Our new server is starting tonight," Toby said.

Mo nodded. He left that stuff to Toby. Mo took care of the food; Toby took care of the people.

"I'm just saying," Toby said, trying for a sneak peek at the menu. "Don't give him a mouthful to recite. He's a white boy."

"Good luck tonight," Mo said, a twisted grin on his face as he passed his back-of-the-receipt notes to Ramon. He did a specials menu every night, with two or three dishes based on what looked interesting at the market that morning.

Toby didn't care what Mo cooked, just as long as he kept making the *injera*, the flat bread that accompanied every dish. It was the foundation of Ethiopian cuisine, the name of their restaurant, and no one made it better than Mo. He could never admit it out loud, but Toby liked Mo's injera better than his mother's.

He was setting up the bar for the night's service when Parvati showed up. She tied on her server's apron and took over, setting tables while Bette finished up her paperwork and got out of their way. Injera was a small restaurant, with only two more servers set to show up: Celeste, who would take Toby's place as host tonight, and Mike, the new kid.

Mike started talking as soon as he arrived, and he didn't stop all night. Toby tried to hide in the kitchen while Mike was clearing tables, but Ramon kicked him out. "We're working in here," he said. Toby escaped behind the bar.

"He's nice," Parvati said, waiting with her tray while Toby got her drinks. "I hope he sticks around."

"If you're looking for a date, stop right there. There will be no fraternization in my restaurant."

She laughed over her shoulder on her way back to her tables. Toby had assigned Mike to the four-top in the window and the two seats in the corner. He was over there now, with his hand on a man's shoulder, and the whole table was laughing along with a joke.

He was good at the job. Toby watched him walk through the restaurant, checking on everyone, not only his tables, before he returned to where Toby was working the bar.

"Having fun?" Toby asked him.

"It's such a nice place," Mike said. He leaned across the bar and spoke in a low voice. "The smell is driving me crazy. I'm starving. How do you stand it?"

Mo did a tasting of the specials for the servers, and he had done a few of the classics for Mike to taste along with them, to get an idea of the whole menu. He said he had never eaten Ethiopian food, but he ate with enthusiasm and had spent much of the night suggesting dishes to customers before they even had a chance to decide.

"You eat before you show up for work," Toby said, deadpan. Mike laughed, so he knew how to take a joke. He was going to get along well at Injera.

"The only thing I have in my fridge right now is beer," he said. He turned away from Toby to glance around the room. Mike was attentive and pleasant to be around. Toby couldn't bring himself to complain about the constant questions. He was new. He had a lot to learn. "What about you?" Mike asked, coming around the bar to grab the cloth and wipe it down for something to do. "Is your wife a good cook?"

It had been a long time since Toby had to come out to someone. He encountered people every day who didn't know, but they didn't always need to know. Mike would find out, and if he was still here when Azzo arrived to take Toby home, he would find out tonight.

"Husband," Toby said, an easy correction.

Mike's mouth fell open, almost comical, but his eyes were also wide, and Toby felt that old, familiar panic reaching up into his throat.

"That's awesome," Mike said. Toby didn't think Mike could be any younger than he already looked. "I have so many questions, man. Where did you meet? How long have you guys been together? Is he hot?"

Toby laughed, but there wasn't time for any of that, of course. As Mike was inching himself closer, Toby spotted a customer glancing around the room.

"Table five," he said. Mike jumped, and he was gone, completely professional once more. He would do well here, Toby decided. He would be a good kid to keep around.

After service, after the chairs were up off the floor and Mike was sweeping, Mo wandered out of the kitchen.

"Kid," he said, loud, so Mike would know who he was talking to. "First night in the restaurant, you have to come out and buy the boys a round."

Mike went pale, the lights from above making him look gaunt.

"Why are you teasing him?" Toby rinsed their glasses and gathered up his things from behind the bar. Azzo should be there any minute. "We want this one to stick around."

"You'll buy a drink for your chef at least," Mo said, stalking across the room and putting an arm around Mike's middle. Mike looked down on Mo—at least a head shorter—with a careful smile. He nodded, like he believed that was the way to keep his job.

"Don't listen to him, Mike." Toby pulled him away from

where Mo was chuckling. He walked Mike to the back, where he put away his broom and picked up his bag. "You don't have to go out tonight. You might want to work your way up to partying with the kitchen guys. They're hard-core."

"Are you coming?" Mike asked. His eyes were big and expectant. He looked so young and made Toby feel so old.

"Azzo's picking me up," Toby said.

"That's your husband? That's a nice name."

Back in the dining room, Mo was at the front door. The lights were off, but Toby could hear his husband laughing. They had their arms around each other, holding each other up as each one bent over with a belly laugh.

"I don't like leaving the two of you alone," Toby said. He shouldered his bag, and Azzo met him halfway, reaching out his hand, like he couldn't bear them apart for one more step. "I think you should make it up to me," he said, putting on his pout for show. Azzo kissed it right off his face.

"Mo said you were flirting," Azzo said, pulling away from the kiss, but he didn't go far. He held Toby in his arms as they swayed and turned around the room.

Toby shook his head. "Mike, you should meet my husband." The kid was nervous. Wiping his hands on his pants, he stepped forward, arm extended in a job-interview handshake. "Our new server, Mike. My husband, Azzo. This is his first night, so be kind."

Azzo asked, "Did you survive, kid?" Mike didn't think; he just nodded. "Do you want to come back tomorrow?" Mike answered that one with another nod, no less certain. "Then you'll do just fine."

"Should we head out?" Mo asked. He had his hand on the door. "Before my staff drinks all night and leaves me with the tab?"

He led the way, holding the door open as Azzo pulled Toby along. Their feet never tangled when they walked this close. They had been walking this close for years. Mike was the last one out, so Toby tossed him the keys to lock up.

"The kid's cute," Azzo said. His voice was low, and his lips brushed Toby's as he spoke. It was half kiss, half question, and Toby leaned into him for more.

"Stop." Toby gave him a smack, then dragged them right back together. Up ahead, Mike was walking with Mo, and it looked like Mo was suffering through the same questions that had dogged Toby all night. "He asked about my wife."

Azzo's laugh made Mo and Mike turn, Mo giving them a fond, knowing look.

"That's adorable. I thought I was the straight one."

"No," Toby said. "You're the butch one. There's a difference." Azzo was built like a football player. It didn't matter that he worked pastry for a living.

"Is he—?" Azzo slowed their steps, putting a little more space between them and their friends ahead. The bar that the Injera staff—actually, most of the restaurant staff on their street—liked best wasn't far. They could walk there after service and stumble home after beer. "I mean, I have my guess, but has he said anything to you?"

"He's gay," Toby said. Mike hadn't, actually, said anything to him, but he was too curious about Toby's relationship to be just another straight college boy. "He didn't say anything, but yeah."

Toby watched them up ahead, Mike turning back to check that he and Azzo were still behind them, flushing and whipping his eyes front when he saw Toby watching.

"Look at that crush," Azzo said, his voice warm against Toby's ear. "He doesn't know what to do with himself."

"What do you want to do with him?" Toby stared over at Azzo. "Should I be worried?"

"Could be fun."

As the crowds grew, closer to the bars and clubs still open at this time of night, they walked apart, then came back together, their hands always tangled, never letting go. Azzo kept Toby on his left side, walking between him and the people standing outside for a smoke.

"Could be fun?" Toby asked, incredulous and too loud over the music and conversation.

"I'm not saying that. Jesus, Toby, what are you saying?"

"You said 'could be fun'!"

Azzo laughed, pressing his forehead to Toby's shoulders, and when Toby put his arms around him, he could feel Azzo shaking with it. "You're so easy." He smacked a kiss on Toby's cheek, wet and loud. "Bet you're thinking about it now."

Someone called their names from the far end of the bar. Toby had to stop to say hi to Veronika behind the bar, and she demanded a kiss from Azzo, too, who didn't often come out with them. Toby went out after service less and less, too. They had done their time, when they were kids, in dingy bars like this.

The back room was quieter, but not by much. The guys from Tanuki brought a huge platter of sushi, and Toby could smell roast chicken. The food at restaurant after-parties was the best.

Josh and Lina, a couple they knew who also worked in separate restaurants, grabbed Azzo's attention. Toby said hi, but they were all pastry chefs, and the conversation quickly turned shop. They held hands, and Toby stood close, pressing his chest to Azzo's side, but he scanned the room, quietly enjoying the excitement between friends after such a long day.

His eyes locked on Mike, leaning back against the bar. Toby gave him a smile. The look on Mike's face wasn't as obvious, and then he turned away. Toby was still watching as he talked to the bartender pulling pints, and when Mike walked their way he had three glasses in his two hands.

"You looked thirsty," he said, letting Toby take the beers from his hands. Toby passed one to Azzo, who raised it in a toast of thanks.

"Keep this one, Toby." Azzo turned fully toward Mike, holding Toby with a hand low on his back, their bodies curved together. "This is your job now," Azzo explained to Mike. "Making sure my neurotic husband doesn't implode by the end of the night."

"Is he prone to doing that?" Mike asked. He took a big gulp of his beer, keeping his face in the glass.

"No," Toby argued. "I'm extremely capable and very professional."

Azzo chuckled deep in his chest. "He's high-strung, and a Saturday night theater crowd will send him hiding in the kitchen."

"I never hide," Toby said, but he admitted to himself that he liked seeing Mike and Azzo getting along, even if it was at his own expense. Their tiny circle of three felt like an island in the big room filled with chefs, cooks, bartenders, servers and the rest of the late night crowd. They were turned and tuned into each other, and the way Mike kept looking the two of them up and down, Toby was ready to invite him somewhere quiet.

"How about coffee?" Azzo said, his beer not even half-empty. Toby was only sipping his. He already felt light-headed, in the stuffy back room, with Azzo holding him so close.

Mike nodded along with Azzo's suggestion. His eyes were glassy and unfocused, but not from the beer, Toby could tell.

He could tell by the way Mike was sure on his feet, but his free hand was rubbing over his thigh, wiping dry his sweaty palms, and when Toby looked down, he saw Mike hard in his trousers.

"There will be more of these parties," Azzo said. "You're not missing much."

He led them both to the bar, where they dropped their glasses. Toby took one more gulp of beer, then they slipped out without saying good-bye. He wasn't ready to explain this to Mo or Josh and Lina or Veronika behind the bar. Toby wasn't sure he could explain this at all.

"This isn't where I thought the night would end up," Mike admitted. "Do you guys do this a lot?"

Azzo laughed, a single bark in the empty alleyway. "We've never done this before."

"We don't have to do this," Toby said. He reached out and took Mike's hand when he said it. "It's just an idea, a bit of a fantasy."

"How long have you two been together?"

Smiling, Azzo pulled Toby back to him. He rubbed his nose over Toby's cheek. "Twenty-two years."

"Jesus," Mike said. He ducked his head, and when he looked back up at them, he grinned and said, "I'm twenty-two."

Azzo's car was about a block away, parked behind his restaurant. He opened the passenger side first, kissing Toby against the open door. Toby was already hardening in his pants, feeling that lovely edge that meant he would get to come soon. When they pulled away from each other's lips, Mike was staring, though he looked away as soon as Toby looked up. He didn't want to be caught, but Toby caught him.

He dragged Mike against the car by the belt around his waist. His steps stuttered into Toby, but his kiss was sure, confident, though the rest of him was nervous. Fingers clenched and released at his sides as Mike leaned into Toby, into the kiss that was moving beyond the first dry press of lips to tongues and teeth and the taste of them both.

"I like it," Azzo said, his hands landing on Mike's shoulders to hold him steady. Azzo kissed him from behind, sucking a mark on the pale expanse of his long neck. Toby leaned back against the door so he could watch. He held on to Mike's belt, sneaking his fingers up under his shirt so he could stroke the soft skin and jumping muscles while Azzo made his mark on Mike. "Let's go home," he said, opening the door and, with his hand on Mike's head, guiding him into the backseat.

When he straightened, Azzo leaned into Toby again, whispering against his lips, "I can't wait."

Toby watched Mike in the rearview mirror. He thought about asking how the kid was doing, but he was calm, his eyes closed, and his head leaned back against the seat. He wasn't asleep. Toby could tell from his breathing, slow and regular, but deliberate. Mike had his fists clenched in the seat on either side of his thighs. He was hanging on for dear life. Toby left him alone, but he was pretty to watch.

They hadn't ever done this before; that much was true. Toby and Azzo had talked about threesomes before. But when you get together in college and stay together for two decades, you don't play the same games that single people do.

He couldn't explain why tonight was the right time, why Mike was the right third, why Toby wanted to do this.

"I'm happy with you," he said, putting his hand on Azzo's on the steering wheel.

"I know," Azzo said, taking a bare second to glance over.

Toby took his hand back. He caught a glimpse of Mike in the backseat, and Mike was looking back. "He is very cute," Toby said, matching grin for grin with his companions in the car.

Azzo laughed. His laugh was the best, the best part of Toby's life, and he heard it every single day.

Toby walked ahead once they were home, opening his own car door before Azzo could do it for him, and leaving the front door ajar for when they decided to join him. He went straight upstairs. An hour ago, Toby didn't know this was going to happen. Now he wanted it. Now he was hard for it. Now he had the time to think about how it would go and what he wanted.

He stripped the covers off the bed and found condoms and lube, tossing them on the pillow. He rinsed his mouth quickly, because there was no time for brushing, stripped his clothes straight into the hamper, and wandered back to the bedroom to find a clean pair of briefs.

Downstairs, he heard the door slam shut. The sound made his cock jerk, and then there were steps on the stairs, and Mike laughing, so different from Azzo. He heard Azzo, too, then the sound was muffled, and Toby knew kissing was happening.

He watched from the doorway, waiting for his husband and their new friend to join him. They were beautiful together, in the way that opposites are beautiful. In color, size, experience, Azzo and Mike were nothing alike. But they fit. Azzo fit his arms around Mike's shoulders, sheltering him from Toby's view, except for those long white arms twined around Azzo's back.

"Toby," Azzo said, bringing Mike to him, like they were being introduced for the first time. "See how hard he is?"

Toby put his hand on Mike's thick cock, still pushing its way out of his foreskin, still growing to its full, proud size. He leaned down to kiss Mike's shoulder, along the line of his collarbone, and down to his pink nipples. He licked them and pulled at them with his teeth until the tight peaks were circled with goose bumps, spreading across Mike's chest as Toby licked his way down further.

"I didn't know," Mike said, shaking his head against Azzo. With his arms crossed over Mike's chest, Azzo continued what Toby started with his nipples. He tweaked them with his big fingers, making Mike gasp and pant. "I didn't know it could feel like this."

"And we're just getting started," Azzo said.

Before that fat cock tempted Toby down to his knees on the hardwood floor, he straightened, grabbed hold of Mike around his hips and dragged them both into the bedroom. They sat on the edge of the bed, Mike between them. He was twitchy, and Toby wondered if it was nerves or arousal.

"Take a breath," Azzo said.

Toby put his hand on Mike's back. "We can stop right here."

"No," he yelped. "I want to do this," he said, nuzzling into Toby like a cat into the hand scratching its head. "I haven't done this before, but I want to do this."

"When you say haven't?" Azzo asked. He had his hand on Mike's thigh, high up, and his fingers were rubbing over the soft inner skin. "You mean this specifically, right? A threesome?"

"Yes," Mike said, turning to smile, a bit shy, at Azzo on his other side. He nuzzled into him, too, and when the nuzzle turned into a kiss, and the kiss turned dirty and deep, the two of them fell back onto the bed. Mike curled into Azzo, leaving his bare ass up for Toby's enjoyment.

The kid was fit, tight like a runner might be, not muscles all over, but not flabby. He was so white, but Toby figured that's how all blonds were, light skin and gorgeous blue eyes. The hair on his legs was so fine and light as to be invisible. It was the same around his hole, which clenched beautifully when Toby pulled his cheeks apart.

"Can I?" he asked. Toby kissed Mike right above the crease, rubbing his nose back and forth, just to see more goose bumps.

He heard Mike's breathy answer above. "Yes," he said into Azzo's chest, muffled, but insistent.

Pressing his face into Mike, Toby pulled a breath deep into his lungs. He swept his tongue wide and flat over the hole, which was desperate to open now. With Azzo taking care of Mike's mouth, Toby focused his attention right here, this one point in the universe, and the tight space beyond.

The lube was right there for him, so Toby squeezed some out onto his fingers, and when his tongue wasn't enough for Mike, he pushed two slick fingers inside. Mike bucked against Azzo, who held him tight around his shoulders.

"More," Azzo told Toby. "The kid wants more."

Toby gave him three fingers. Then Toby twisted those fingers, up and at an angle, and he found the button he was looking for. When Toby added another finger, the keening noise Mike made was almost too much. He almost made Toby come, pulsing around his fingers and sucking him farther inside.

Azzo was moving up the bed. He was still wearing his shirt, though it was unbuttoned now. He was the last of them still clothed, and now Azzo guided Mike's head down to his fly, encouraging the kid to go exploring.

Toby was all ready to fuck him, but there was a delicious scene happening in front of him. His husband on his back, hands in Mike's hair, and that big cock of his just poking out of his boxer shorts, through the open fly of his jeans. He watched Azzo's face as Mike sucked him down, watched for the surprise and the pleasure, Azzo's tongue caught between his teeth, and his eyes rolling back.

"He's good," Toby said. "Isn't he good, Az?" With his fingers still inside Mike, Toby matched the rhythm, pushing in when

Mike sucked down, taking Azzo's hard cock all the way into his throat. Toby pulled his fingers out, teasing the rim of Mike's hole, when Mike dragged his mouth off, until only his lips were touching the dripping head of the erection he held with both hands. They kept that up, moving syrup slow because that's how Azzo liked it and that's how Toby guided Mike.

"Pass me a condom?" Toby had to finally remove his fingers because he couldn't do this left-handed. He stroked a gentle hand over Mike's back as he eased his fingers out, all four of them, and he felt a shiver when Mike made the most glorious moan around Azzo's cock.

He was quick to rip the foil open with his teeth, roll the condom down on his own erection that was demanding some attention, and use his already-slick fingers to prepare his cock. Mike's hole was ready, too, opening and closing like a hungry mouth as the younger man's hips moved against the bed.

Toby draped himself over Mike's back, sucking a kiss on the back of his neck and riding his up-and-down rhythm on Azzo's cock. "You're doing so good, baby," he said, scraping his teeth over the curve of Mike's ear. "Listen to him groan. Azzo loves your mouth, Mike."

Hands on Mike's shoulders, Toby pushed himself up to reach Azzo's mouth. He wanted to taste those grunts and groans for himself. Toby mashed their lips together, opening his mouth wide when Azzo pushed his tongue inside. "Okay," Toby said, his voice rough with arousal, wavering like his cock, pressed between Mike's asscheeks. "I'm going to fuck him now."

Azzo said, "Yes, fuck him now."

For all they had talked about this particular fantasy, Toby never believed it would happen. Finding himself here, in bed with his husband, this eager twenty-two-year-old between them, Toby needed a moment to think. He ran his hand down Mike's back, tracing the goose bumps and feeling how Mike's muscles jumped as Toby touched him. He was real. He was young. He was choking on Azzo's cock, and he wanted Toby to fuck him.

"Sit up, baby," Toby said. He grabbed Mike around his hips and eased him back, off Azzo, onto his haunches to sit back against Toby's chest. Toby's cock was ready, pressing up against Mike's ass. "You're okay," he said, rubbing a comforting hand over Mike's belly. He was panting, with his head resting on Toby's shoulder. "Tell me you want this."

"I want this," Mike said, no hesitation in his voice, just the rough, used sound of a cocksucking throat. "I want this," Mike said, more forcefully. "Fuck me."

Toby had to fuck him. He reached down between their bodies, grasping himself at the base and guiding his slick and condom-covered cock into Mike, straight up. It was one easy push, and they were joined. Mike's hand flailed at his side before Azzo caught him, pressed in close to hold Mike between their chests, and he put Mike's hands on his cock to finish the job. Azzo was still hard, Mike was panting in his ear, and Toby set them a rhythm like breathing.

In and out, until Mike was bouncing in his lap, squeezing his ass around Toby's cock to make it good and opening himself up to make it deep. Toby put his mouth on Mike from behind, just trying to hang on, make it last. He couldn't believe how long the kid could go.

Mike made Azzo come first, folding his body into a beautiful curve to put his mouth on Azzo's cock and swallow down his orgasm. Toby held his husband's hand through it all, and he felt when it was too much and when Azzo was ready to let go. He felt Azzo come into the body between them.

Toby took his time, digging his teeth into Mike's shoulder when his orgasm rushed inside him. Mike was stroking his own cock, whimpering, dragging himself to the finish line, like he was the only one who would, like Toby and Azzo wouldn't be there to take care of him.

"I'll get you there," Toby said. He thrust his hips up as he pulled Mike back into his lap, driving his cock deeper. He wanted to get Mike there first. Toby wanted to feel him around his cock. Toby didn't want to come until Mike was shouting out his orgasm and squeezing himself around Toby's cock.

The feel of it, that tight passage, sucking Toby inside and holding him there. Mike was holding them together, and Toby did the same, one arm across Mike's chest and the other, his hand on Mike's hand, pulling until Mike had nothing left to shoot, until Azzo's heaving chest was splattered with come, until Toby let out a roar against Mike's skin and came, too, deep inside Mike's ass.

Limp, heavy and tired, Toby guided them down onto the bed next to where Azzo was still recovering. Mike lay between them, cradled with Toby's cock in his ass and Azzo's hands in his hair.

"That was new," Azzo said, because he was the only one who could wrap his mouth around words. Mike laughed, and Toby felt it in his own body, almost too much, like another orgasm too soon. He pulled his cock out and flopped, sweaty, on his side of the bed. Azzo had Mike in his arms now, brushing his fingers through his hair and asking soft questions Toby could barely hear.

Mike was saying, "Yes," and "Yeah," and "I do," and Toby agreed. He didn't know what this was, but with his husband in their bed beside him, this boy in their bed between them, Toby thought another round might be fun.

THE ROAD TRIP

Kitten Boheme

S top!" I swatted Finn's hand away from my face.

"What?" Finn looked at me innocently.

"I'm trying to drive! Do you want us to get there alive?"

Finn groaned and sunk down deep into his seat. "At this point I don't care!"

I took my eyes off the road long enough to shoot a glare in his direction. "This road trip was your idea."

"I'm bored."

"What are you? Three?"

"Are we there yet?"

I raised an eyebrow and looked over at him. He grinned back at me.

A few months ago Finn announced that for our five-year anniversary of being a couple we should get out of our little upstate New York apartment and see more of the world. *Great,* I thought, *we can finally use our frequent flyer miles and book a vacation to Hawaii.* But no, he thought we should see America the old-fashioned way—by car.

I reached over and smacked him on the knee. "Behave yourself."

He grabbed my hand and threaded his fingers through mine; lifting it to his mouth he planted a kiss on the back of my hand. "I love you."

"Yeah, yeah, yeah."

I wanted to be mad at him; we had spent the last sixteen hours in the car and had had a terrible night's sleep in some sketchy roadside motel. I was edging on my last nerve, but then he looked at me with those baby blues of his and instantly all was forgiven—the bad coffee, the drive-through meals and every roadside tourist trap he made us stop at between New York and Minnesota.

"All right, I may just love you too." I confessed.

"I know," he chirped, giving my hand a quick squeeze.

We sat in silence for some time, enjoying the chatter of NPR and the constant hum of the road beneath us.

"Oh my god!" Finn yelled, his face pressed against the passenger window, his breath fogging the glass.

I slammed on the brakes and the car just behind had to swerve around us, the driver laying on his horn and gesturing rudely as he drove by.

"What? What's wrong?" I panicked.

"We should eat there!" He pointed excitedly to a roadside café.

"Seriously? That's what you nearly got us killed for?" My heart had leapt up into my throat; I tried to swallow it back down.

Finn just looked back at me, unaware or uncaring of what just happened. He shrugged, "I'm hungry."

"You are always hungry." I rubbed his slightly less than six-pack gut. He returned my mock affection with a punch to the arm. I laughed. "Fine, let's stop." I relented, flipping on my turn signal and pulling in to the café.

I parked our Chevy station wagon, bought especially for this trip. "See the USA in your Chevrolet" was Finn's mantra. Being the pushover I am, I relented and traded in my Audi for this 1980s monstrosity.

As I unbuckled my seat belt I leaned over. "You owe me. Big." I puckered my lips and waited.

Finn closed the gap between us and pressed his mouth to mine.

I melted into his kiss, the moistness of his lips, the heat of his breath and the familiar feel of his tongue sliding against mine. Five years and he still can make me weak at the knees with just a kiss. We clung eagerly to each other and a hand slid up the nape of my neck, fingers curling in my hair. I shuddered. I put my hand against his face, the fleshy pad of my thumb caressing his cheekbone. When the kiss broke Finn left a trail of soft kisses from the corner of my mouth to my ear. He breathed deep and heavy in my ear, a chill ran down my body and I could feel something beginning to stir in my pants. He whispered, "I want a bacon cheeseburger."

I pushed him away from me, stifling a laugh. "Get away from me."

"Come on, let's go eat." Finn reached over and pulled the keys from the ignition. "I'm buying."

"Damn right you are." I reached for the door handle.

"Wait!" Finn held up a hand, motioning for me to stop. He jumped out of the car, hustled over to the driver's side and opened the door for me. It was a silly thing he did, ever since our first date. He thought it was romantic and I humored him, although the tradition has grown on me.

"Thank you, babe." I took his outstretched hand and lifted

myself out of the seat with a groan. It felt good to finally stretch my legs. Finn linked his arm through mine and started pulling me toward the entrance and grudgingly I followed.

The café was little more than a greasy spoon attached to a defunct gas station. I'm sure it had seen better days, but judging from the crumbling, fading exterior, those days were long past.

"Hello darlins!" We were greeted by a perky young waitress in a blue dress and apron. "Just have yourselves a seat anywhere; I'll be right with you!"

"Just any old where?" Finn mocked in an equally enthusiastic high-pitched squeal.

"Uh-huh!" the waitress said, nodding.

I gave Finn a quick jab in the ribs with my elbow, stifling a snicker.

We picked out a booth in the far corner of the room and sat down. The waitress, whose name tag read TANYA, tossed a couple of menus in front of us. "Would you like to hear our specials?"

"Nope." Finn shook his head; he already had his heart set on a bacon cheeseburger and would not be swayed.

"Let's hear them," I coaxed.

"We have a Reuben sandwich with chips for $4.99. The soup of the day is baked potato and the pie is...umm." Scrunching up her face she looked up at the ceiling. She was silent for a moment, lost in deep thought. "Hey, Merle!" she yelled, making both Finn and me jump in our seats. "What's the pie special today?"

A large, greasy man, who I could only presume to be Merle, leaned out of the order window. "Chocolate cream," he shouted back to Tanya.

"What?" she screamed back at him.

"Chocolate cream!" Merle bellowed to the waitress.

"Oh yeah!" She turned her attention back to Finn and me, both of us now sitting sheepishly in our booth. "The pie special today is chocolate cream pie." She smiled innocently.

"I'm just going to have a bacon cheeseburger with fries and a large cherry coke," Finn said, handing her back the unopened menu.

"Sure thing, honey. For you, sir?" She turned to me.

I panicked; I hadn't had a chance to even crack open the sticky plastic-coated menu. I quickly opened it and darted through it, while Tanya tapped her pen impatiently against her order book.

"Do you need another minute?"

"No!" I quickly pointed to the first thing I saw. "I'll have that." I leaned in close to read what I was pointing at. "I'll have the ladies' waistline-watching salad."

"Mmm-kay." Tanya wrote down my order, her pencil scratching judgmentally across the paper. She turned on her heels and skipped back to the order window, depositing the slip with Merle.

I looked up across the table at Finn; he was staring back at me with an eyebrow cocked. "What?" I mouthed.

"Watching your waistline are you?"

"Shut up, you know what happens when I panic." I sighed heavily. "And I was really looking forward to some onion rings too."

Finn instantly shot his hand up in the air and waved it around for Tanya's attention.

"Yes, sugar?"

"Can we get a side of onion rings too?" he called back.

"Sure thing!"

"There, better?" He brushed a hand over my face and through my hair.

I nodded.

Our food arrived. Finn finished his meal in record time and began sneaking food from my plate when he thought I wasn't looking. "Would you like the rest?" I asked. I was still surprisingly full from our last roadside meal anyway.

He looked longingly at what was left of my onion rings. "Naw, you go ahead and finish."

"I need to watch my waistline anyway." I pointed to my salad then grabbed at my stomach, pinching a little extra flab between my fingers.

"You look amazing," he cooed as he reached for a fistful of onion rings.

Like a carrion bird swooping in on fresh road kill, Tanya was suddenly hovering over our empty plates. "Can I get ya'll anything else? Pie? Coffee?"

"Pie. A la mode," Finn mumbled through his last mouthful of food. I grimaced as bits of onion ring fell out of his mouth and looked up apologetically at our waitress. She just smiled back; a true hardened veteran of the truck stop service world, she had seen it all.

"And for you, hun?"

"Just coffee and the bill."

"Have that for you in two shakes of a lamb's tail!" She flounced away.

I leaned across the table and motioned Finn to come in closer. "I need to use the little boy's room."

Finn sat back, snorting and rolling those baby blues at me. Having been born in rural backwater Mississippi he lacked the sense of refinement I imagined I had. "Are you asking my permission, buttercup?" he mocked.

"Maybe I am," I countered, clasping my hands together pleadingly. "Please, sir, I really have to go," I begged, imagining myself akin to poor Oliver, begging for another bowlful of gruel.

"Go."

"Oh thank you, sir!" I grabbed his hand and kissed it worshipfully. "Thank you!"

"You are so weird. Go pee!" Finn shooed me away from our table, snickering.

I pulled myself up out of the booth and wandered to the end of the diner, where an old backlit sign hung on the wall: RE T OOMS. I followed the sign down a dimly lit hallway and found the men's room. It was surprisingly clean; I had half expected raw sewage, leaky pipes, and messages calling for help scrawled across the walls in blood. There were two stalls in the room; I pushed open the door to one of the stalls and sat down, letting out a long sigh of relief after a minute or two.

"That good, huh?"

The voice startled me out of my momentary state of bliss. I looked around and caught a blue eye staring back at me through a silver-dollar-sized hole.

"Holy shit, Finn!" I jumped, my heart leaping into my throat for a second time that day.

"What do you think this is for?" He wiggled a finger at me through the hole in the bathroom stall wall.

"What the hell are you doing in here?"

"What? Do I need your permission to take a piss?" He put his eye back to the hole and ogled me.

"I'll poke your eye out," I threatened.

"Do you think it's what I think it is?"

"What *what* is?" Not really caring what he was talking about, I fumbled for a sheet of toilet paper.

"What this is." His eye disappeared, to my relief. I heard the rasping sound of his zipper and a moment later his thick, fleshy member slid through the hole.

I gasped, blushing like some sort of virginal schoolboy. "Finn! What on earth..." I couldn't even finish my thought.

"Come on," he goaded. "Don't be so uptight. Remember how you said you wanted to add some role-play to our bedroom... you can pretend we've never met.... We are two lonely travelers, out on the dusty road, who just happened to stop at the same diner, looking for a little bit of pie and hoping for some action."

"Don't be ridiculous," I scolded, but I kept staring at his cock. I knew every inch of it, every throbbing vein, but somehow, through this faceless hole, it looked unknown. He was just a stranger thrusting his horny manhood through the hole fishing for action, like a fisherman with a worm on a hook. I felt my own manhood twitch.

I knelt down on the tiled floor in front of his dick. I grasped it in one hand, rubbing it from tip to shaft. I ran my thumb in circles around the head, spreading around the trickle of precome that had just begun to collect around his slit. I heard him groan from the other side of the wall; he pushed his cock deeper through the hole begging for more of my touch. I sat back and eyed his dick once more; reaching down, I unzipped my pants and pulled my own cock out. I began stroking my length, my eye on Finn, watching his cock shudder in anticipation of my next move.

There was a gentle knock on the stall wall. "Did you fall asleep in there?" Finn questioned, his breath heavy with excitement.

"Are you in a hurry?" I teased. He just answered me with a long moan.

I put my warm, wet tongue on the head of his penis and licked. Finn sighed his approval. I slid my tongue slowly down the underside of his shaft, lingering there for a moment before working my way back up to the tip. Suddenly, I was hit with a sense of urgency, my own cock, hard and aching, begging for relief. I wrapped my lips around him and begin sucking furiously, as if it would relieve my own burning desires. Finn moaned in agreement with my sudden change of pace, his hips rocking against the stall wall, causing it to shake and shudder like the room was having an orgasm of its own.

I loved the feeling of his dick in my mouth, the smooth silk of his shaft sliding along my tongue, the swollen head hitting the back of my throat. It was almost more than he could bear, and I could feel Finn beginning to tense up; I knew he was ready to come. I backed off, slowing my pace; I wanted to savor the moment, and I wasn't ready for this to be over quite yet.

"Don't stop," he pleaded through the wall. "Please, don't stop."

I stroked my hand down his shaft, adding to his agony. Again he begged me for more, but I didn't relent. I knew that the thrill of the buildup was his favorite part. My fingers traced coyly around his swollen head and down the sides of his dick, still slick with my spit. Finally, I was the one who couldn't take it anymore; I wanted his juicy cock again. I swallowed his cock, pushing it deep into my throat, taking in as much of him as I could. I pulled back—my tongue rolling around him, up and down his shaft, over the head—then pushed back down, taking in as much of his delicious manhood as I could.

"I'm going to come," Finn gasped out.

I opened my mouth wide, letting him shoot his load into my mouth. Once more, I wrapped my lips around his member and made sure to suck and lick every last drop out of him. Before I was ready, he pulled his dick away from the hole, and a moment later it was replaced by his mouth.

"Fuck me," he said.

Those words made my dick snap to throbbing attention. I stood up quickly when I heard the adjacent stall door unlock. I quickly unlocked my own door and stepped out. Finn stood in front of me, pants around his ankles and a hungry grin on his face. I teased my manhood and smiled back. Finn then reached out to lock the bathroom door. "No!" I shouted, pushing his body hard against the wall with my own. "Leave it unlocked." He looked at me, surprised by my sudden kinky streak. The thought of someone walking in, of us being caught in the act, thrilled me beyond belief.

My gaze caught his, and I pushed myself closer to him, our lips meeting for a slow passionate kiss, all of our longing and need appeased for just a moment. In that moment it was just me and the man I have loved for the last five years, no diner, no old Chevy, no waitress—just Finn, myself and this kiss.

I was shaken from my bliss by a hand forcefully grabbing my crotch. Finn licked his lips.

"Fuck me," he said again, shaking loose of my hold on him and turning around, pushing his ass up in the air for me. I stepped forward, pushing the head of my penis against his ass. I spit on my hand and slid it between his asscheeks, moistening his tight hole. I slipped a finger in, then a second and third, loosening up his asshole, teasing him, getting him ready for my cock.

Finn leaned against the wall, balancing himself on one forearm as he reached his free hand down between his legs so he could stroke my erect cock. I eased my cock into his opening, then there was a staggering wave of pleasure running through me as I sunk my cock slowly into his ass.

Finn grunted as I slid inside. He pushed against me, forcing more of me into his tight passage. I placed my hands on his hips to steady myself and give myself leverage. I started picking up the pace, thrusting hard and deep, pulling myself almost all the way out before watching my shaft disappear again into his ass. His grunts quickly turned to moans as he tried to brace himself against the wall, still pushing back, meeting me with every thrust. "Fuck," he moaned. "Fuck. Fuck!" He was a man of few words. My balls banged against his, like a perverse Newton's cradle. Every time we connected I felt a chill run up my body and down to the tip of my throbbing cock. I knew it was my turn to come and so did Finn, and once again he reached around, this time grabbing my balls, holding them, pulling on them, stretching the skin gently. This put me over the edge; with a final thrust I groaned my way through a mind-blowing orgasm. I stood there for a moment, catching my breath before I slowly let myself slide out, come still dripping. I smiled, then began to chuckle.

"Well, that was unexpected."

Finn reached down around his ankles, fishing for his jeans. Catching them by the waistband, he pulled them up. I watched, a little disappointed, as his manhood disappeared underneath the denim.

"I told you this looked like a good place to stop and eat." He gave me one of his impish grins.

I rolled my eyes. "You are nothing but trouble, sir."

His grin just widened as he held open the bathroom door for me. "What do you say we get out of here and find a nice comfy hotel for the night?"

"One with more than one star and a working toilet?"

"And little to no mice," he added.

I clutched my chest. "Be still my beating heart. You sure know how to woo a man."

Returning to the diner, I began to feel a little sheepish. I couldn't believe we had just done what we had, in a public restroom no less. Finn grabbed ahold of my hand and pulled me toward the door.

Tanya stepped out from behind the counter. "Hey! Don't you boys want your pie?" she asked, pointing to our vacated table where a lonely slice of pie sat in a melting pool of vanilla ice cream.

"No thanks!" Finn said, dropping a wad of cash by the cash register as we ran for the door. "That should cover the bill!" he called back. We bolted across the parking lot like a pair of jackrabbits, exhilarated by our tryst.

"I'll drive!" Finn exclaimed as he slid awkwardly across the hood of our car like it was the General Lee.

"Fine, shotgun!" I called back, sliding far more gracefully into the passenger side.

We sat in our old Chevy and looked at each other in silence. Maybe this road trip wouldn't be so bad after all. I leaned in to plant a kiss on Finn. Just before our lips met he let out a loud, cheeseburger-scented burp.

"Mmm. Just as tasty the second time around!" He licked his lips to illustrate.

I sat back in my seat. Then again, there was still another thousand miles to go. At least there were plenty of diners between here and California.

NEVER
TOO LATE

Oleander Plume

I was at the mall again, using my gold card to drown my sorrows. So far, I had purchased a cashmere sweater, a pair of sinfully tight jeans and some skimpy red underwear. While I was heading out to my car, a shop that offered ear piercing caught my eye. I tugged my earlobe as I peered in the window. Tony had always wanted me to get it pierced, but I refused out of fear. As I stood there, a fantasy grew in my head. I would waltz in the door, earlobe sparkling. Tony would swoon, then carry me off to bed and pound me into the mattress. Deep down, I knew there was zero chance of that happening, but I went inside anyway. I perused the selection of earrings while a preteen girl with pigtails stared at me.

"You're getting an earring?" Her mother turned to glare at me.

"Maybe."

"You're a boy."

"Yes, but I'm a pirate. All pirates have earrings."

"A pirate? Cool!" Big eyes from Pigtails, another glare from Mommy.

The teenager behind the counter had a name tag that said BRITNI. She chomped her gum with a bored expression on her face.

"Which ear?"

"Does it matter?" She shrugged. "How about the left one?"

Britni made a dot on my earlobe with a purple pen, then handed me a small mirror.

"Is this position okay?"

I caught a glimpse of myself in the mirror and cringed. Forty-year-old man in a store targeted for little girls, no wonder Mommy gave me the stink eye. All at once the fine lines around my eyes became apparent, along with a few gray hairs. I wondered if the mall had a Botox kiosk.

"It's fine." I passed her back the mirror. "How bad is this going to hurt?"

"Really bad, but just for a second."

"Thank you for your honesty. Go ahead, puncture me."

A few seconds later, I had a six-carat cubic zirconia glittering on my earlobe. Britni smiled for the first time.

"It looks really good on you."

As much as I enjoyed her compliment, it made me melancholy, since I hadn't gotten one from Tony in months.

When I arrived home, he was still at the office, no surprise there. Lately, all he did was work. It was like I was living with a ghost. While I waited for him, I took a shower, put on my new undies and nothing else. Finally, at 7:30, he stomped in. He gave me a nod as he tossed his briefcase on the bed and loosened his tie.

"Baby, you're home!" I tried to wrap myself around him but he nudged me away.

"I need to take a quick shower, I have a conference call from Japan in thirty minutes."

"Notice anything different about me?" I tossed my hair back.

"You're in your underwear. Put some pants on."

"Want some help in the shower?" I said to Tony's back while he headed for the bathroom.

"Not tonight."

"You said that yesterday."

The door closed and the conversation was over. I crawled into bed with a pint of Häagen-Dazs and a spoon, feeling defeated.

"Oh, rocky road, you never let me down."

I kissed the ice-cream carton, then proceeded to devour the contents. It hadn't always been like this. Tony and I had lived together for fifteen years. In the beginning, we were blissfully happy, spending every spare minute together, usually naked. Everything was wonderful until about five years ago. That's about the time his small company took off and became the monster that it now was, gobbling up each spare minute of Tony's life. I was not even sure what he did; all I knew was that he made a ton of money, most of which he spent on me. I can't lie, I love having expensive things, but I'd give it all up for one hour alone with him.

I finished my ice cream about the same time he finished his call. He came to bed, tense and moody.

"Are you done for the night?"

"No. I'm going to rest for ten minutes, then I have some paperwork to take care of."

"Maybe you should hire another assistant." Tony gave me the "You're a dumb ass" look. I hate that look. "So, ten minutes, I can think of a lot of things we could do in ten minutes."

"Not now, Braiden."

"It would relax you." I tugged at the waistband of his sweat-pants, longing for a taste of him, no matter how brief. He pushed my hand away.

"Please don't, I'll want to sleep after that."

I pushed his hair out of his eyes. "What would you like to do?"

He slid down until he was flat on his back. "I want to rest for ten minutes." His dark eyes closed. "In silence."

"Fine. I'll make myself scarce."

I grabbed the empty ice-cream container and headed down-stairs to the kitchen, still clad in only my underwear. I caught a glimpse of myself in one of the French doors, and wondered why he didn't want to touch me anymore. Sure, I was forty, but I kept in shape. I worked a full-time job and paid my share of the expenses. That's when the horrible thought hit me. Tony must be cheating. My body turned to cold lead and possible suspects came to mind. Jeffrey, his personal assistant, fresh out of college and blond. Tony liked blonds. Or, maybe he was seeing Richard, his second in command. Richard had an ass you could spend all day nibbling on.

I dashed back upstairs, intent on confronting him, but he was sound asleep. I stretched out beside him and played with his dark curls. He had a few gray hairs, too, but wore them better than me. Tony was one of those guys who only grows sexier with age. I traced his lips, so full and dark against his bronzed skin, and tried to remember the last time he'd kissed me. I certainly couldn't remember the last time we'd fucked. Sure, I gave Tony a blow job now and again, but I had to beg first. It took him forever to shoot his load, and when I was finished, my lips were swollen and my tonsils felt bruised. But I always savored the taste of him afterward, while I lay there in the dark, pressed up against his warm body.

I could have been the one to stray; I had plenty of offers, but I loved him too much, so I stayed faithful. Unless you count Big Red, the vibrator I've had since college. When Tony was away and I couldn't take the emptiness, Big Red was there to fill me up, for a little while anyway. Sometimes, I would pretend it was Tony's cock, fucking me the way he used to, with his sexy growl humming against my ear.

Another week went by. This time, I got a new haircut. I'd worn my hair shoulder length since college, and now I finally lopped it all off. My hairdresser cut it extremely short in the back, but left it long in the front, swept forward into my eyes. He said it made me look sexy, and ten years younger. It also showed off my new earring.

I couldn't wait for Tony to get home from work; I was sure my new look would get his attention. I met him at the door and waited for him to notice.

"Hey, babe, I have to take a shower and pack. I have a flight to Chicago in two hours."

He brushed past me and headed upstairs. I skulked into the kitchen and ate a carton of rocky road, right over the sink. And I cried. I was still eating it when he came back downstairs. He stood in the kitchen and stared at me, as if about to say something when a car honked outside.

"There's my limo. You okay?"

"Sure, I'm fucking peachy."

"See you on Sunday."

"Yeah. Sunday."

Fueled by sugar, I ransacked his office, searching for clues of his infidelity, but came up empty. Undaunted, I thumbed through his desk calendar and found out where he was staying, then booked a flight of my own. I cried as I packed a bag, wondering what I would do if I really caught him with another man.

I was tied up in knots for the entire flight, my stomach cramping over what I might find. The trip seemed to take forever, but I finally arrived at his hotel room around 9:30 p.m. He was surprised to see me, and pretty annoyed.

"What are you doing here?" Tony's face was flushed and his tie was askew.

"I missed you. Can't I at least come in for a while?"

His suite was large and tastefully decorated. A small glass of whiskey sat on the coffee table untouched. The bed looked like an office supply store had thrown up all over it.

"I'm expecting a conference call in about five minutes. Maybe you can sit over there and watch TV or something."

"And stay out of the way?"

"Sure."

The fact that he wasn't overjoyed to see me broke my heart, but at least he was alone. I halfheartedly watched a movie in the living area while Tony sprawled out on the bed, up to his eyeballs in business transactions. I could hear the tension in his voice amidst the frantic shuffling of papers and clicking of keystrokes. When he finished his call, I picked up the glass of whiskey and offered it to him.

"Thanks." He knocked it back in one swallow.

"Better?"

"Not really."

I traced his crotch with one finger. "I could take some of your tension away."

"Not now, Braiden."

"Later?"

"See this stack? I have to read this entire file tonight, for a meeting I have tomorrow afternoon. I'll probably be up until two as it is. In case you haven't noticed, I don't have time for any fun and games."

His phone rang again, and he scowled when he glanced at the screen. I slunk back into the living room while he took the call. While I listened in, it all became clear. Tony was miserable, but not because of me. His job was killing him.

"Listen, Robert, I told you on Wednesday, the company is not for sale. Yeah, well, you would sound stressed, too, if you were me. Sure. Right. Look, I have to go. Bye." Tony groaned and tossed the phone aside.

"Someone wants to buy you out?"

"Robert Langford offered me four million."

I sat on the bed. "Why didn't you take it?"

"Why would you want me to?" He looked stunned.

"Tell me something, are you happy?"

"Sure, I'm happy. How can you ask such a ridiculous question?" His phone rang again and I shoved it under a pillow. "What are you doing?"

"I want your full attention for five minutes. Can you give me five minutes?"

He glared at me while he nodded and held up five fingers. When I spoke, the tears started, no matter how hard I tried to blink them back.

"I can tell you're miserable. Why not sell the business? You would be free."

"I can't sell, what would we do for money?"

"Are you fucking kidding me? You couldn't live for the rest of your life on four million? Besides, I still work you know. The ad agency pays pretty well."

"I could live on four million, but I don't think you could."

"What?"

"I know how you like to live. That's why I do all this, to keep you happy."

"You think I'm some shallow gold digger?"

He stood up and grabbed the bottle of whiskey. "For fuck sake, Braiden, you go through money like it's water. Parties, clothes, Italian shoes. You can't tell me that shit doesn't make you happy." He tipped more liquor into his glass. "Ask yourself a question, could you give that up?"

"Yes."

"Yes?"

"I can't lie, being rich is fun, But not at the expense of our relationship. Do you even love me anymore?"

"Of course I love you, more than anything."

"When was the last time we made love? Can you remember? How long has it been since we kissed, or snuggled in front of the TV?"

"Jesus, Braiden, snuggle? Kiss? I barely have time to breathe." Both phones rang at the same time. "Fuck! You know, I don't even know who I am anymore. It's like I'm not even me; I am the company, or a robot. I don't remember when we kissed, or had sex, or even smiled at each other." He gestured toward the mess on the bed. "This is all I know, it's my life. Right here, Braiden, this is my whole fucking life."

He sank to the floor and began to sob. I crouched down and put my arms around him.

"Sell it."

"I wish I could, I can't take it anymore. There's a hole in my stomach the size of Texas, and I miss you, baby, I miss you so much."

"Tony, I love you, more than anything. I could live in a cave with you, as long as we're happy, none of the material things matter. Remember when we first met? I was a starving artist and you had just graduated college? All we had in our cabinets were cans of soup, the cheap kind. But we were so happy."

He pulled back and stared at me; his face was wet. "You deserve more than cheap canned goods, I want to give you the best." He stroked my cheek. "Braiden, you're forty years old, and you still look like you did when we first met, like a fashion model. Everyone wanted you, I still can't believe you picked me. All I want is to give you the world."

"I don't want the world, Tony, I only want you. Call Robert. Right now."

"Are you sure?"

I kissed him and felt a dam open up. His fingers twisted into my hair and his tongue danced against mine. "Baby," he murmured against my lips, "I forgot how sweet you taste. And I love your hair this way, I noticed, I just didn't take the time to tell you."

"What about this?" I pointed to my earring.

"Okay, that I didn't notice. Damn, it's so sexy, I love it." He kissed my earlobe.

I found his phone and pressed it into his hand. He leaned back against the bed and stretched his legs out, then smiled at me while he dialed.

"Robert, make it five mil, and you've got a deal."

I could hear Robert shrieking on the other end. "Five million?"

"Yeah, take it or leave it."

"I'll take it. My lawyer will work on a contract right away. How quickly can you get to New York?"

Tony gazed into my eyes. "I'm not going anywhere tonight. I can probably get a flight out in the morning. Does that work for you?"

"Absolutely. This is fantastic news, Tony. You're not going to back out are you?"

He picked up my hand and kissed the back of it. "No way.

This is a done deal. Write it up." Tony hung up the phone, then tossed it aside. "I'm free."

"How do you feel?"

"Hornier than a teenage boy." I jumped to my feet and started clearing off the bed. "Yeah, let's get rid of all this." He powered down his laptops, I moved all the paperwork to the desk.

"We can buy a smaller place, and I can sell my car."

"I just sold the company for five million. Keep the car."

He grabbed me and kissed my lips as he pushed me back on the bed. I dug my heels into his back and ground my cock against his. The heat between us roared back to life, igniting us both until I thought we might burn alive.

"Fuck me, right now. No foreplay, just get up in me."

"I need a shower."

"Tony, please, I need it so bad. There's lube in my suitcase." I felt like I would die if I didn't get his cock inside. My clothes flew in all directions, but Tony just unzipped and pulled out his dick; it was harder than I had seen it in years.

"Braiden, my balls feel like they're going to explode."

His hands were shaking when he greased up his dick. I pulled my legs back. Tony licked his lips while he stared between my legs.

"It's still so pretty; fuck, I'm so hard."

"Tony, hurry."

"Yeah, yeah, here it comes, baby, I can't wait either."

I groaned as he pushed in. It had been a while, but I loosened up quickly. This was what I had been craving, the feel of his hardness mingled with my softness. To be one with him, joined in mutual satisfaction. His cock spread me open wide when he drove in deep. Tony growled.

"That's it, the sound I've been wanting to hear. That sex growl you always make."

He did it again, and I got goose bumps all over when it rumbled from his throat.

"Sweet angel, you're so tight."

"Keep talking." I wanted him in every way, to hear his voice, to feel his body, to smell his male musk, to taste his lips, to see the lust in his eyes, all for me. "Tell me more."

"You feel so good, so hot. Squeeze me between your legs like you used to." I wrapped my thighs around his hips. "Yeah, you own me when you latch on to me like that."

"I never knew you felt that way." Tears welled up again.

"I should have told you more often. I figured you knew already. How can you be this beautiful and not know? You're perfect."

I grabbed his tie and pulled him close for a kiss. It caused his dick to drive in deeper and I gasped. A twinge of pain, but I welcomed it. The ecstasy that followed made it all worthwhile. He rubbed up against my prostate, sending me over the edge.

"You're coming? I didn't even touch you."

I arched my back and almost had a seizure, the orgasm was so intense. "Tony." His name came out more like a sex noise than an actual word. He gripped my ass and buried himself deep, almost more than I could take, I was so sensitive after coming so hard. But he quickly unleashed inside me, a relief for the both of us.

"Sweet Jesus, I needed you so bad," Tony mumbled against my neck after he flopped down on top of me. He slipped his cock out. I tried to clench and keep it inside, but I lacked the strength.

"Put it back."

"Uh-uh. We're going to take a shower, then I'm going to lick you from your eyebrows down to your toes and everywhere in between, and I mean everywhere."

"Promise?"

"Promise."

Tony took my hand and dragged me to the bathroom. The shower was large enough for both of us, and seeing it filled my head with kinky ideas. He turned on the water and felt it with his hand.

"It's cold, wait a few minutes." I was still giddy with the afterglow, and dripping with jizz down to my knees. Tony noticed and laughed. "Damn, baby, I filled you up good."

"It was amazing, Tony."

He leaned in for a kiss and my heart burst. It felt like we had turned back the clock. His huge smile reminded me of the night we met. At a friend's party, I spotted him from across the room and the world stopped. Two hours later, I had him in my bed, and swore I would never, ever let him go.

I watched him take off his clothes. His body was a little thicker in the middle, but he still took my breath away. Tony is covered in thick muscle and a nice layer of body fat, wrapped up in bronzed skin that's hairy in all the right places. I squeezed his pecs; they filled my hands with hunky goodness.

"I'm going on a diet and joining a gym."

"Nonsense, you're my big teddy bear."

"Well, this big teddy bear needs to lose about twenty pounds." He pulled me into warm spray and rubbed shower gel all over me. "You're still so slender, how do you do it?"

"I masturbate a lot." Tony laughed and slapped my ass. "Yes, more of that, lots more."

"What have you been reading? Don't tell me you're into the BDSM scene."

"A little spanking never hurt anyone, but I don't want you to tie me up or pull my hair when I'm sucking your dick. Ew." I poured soap on my hands and grabbed Tony's cock, turning it frothy. "Let me wash you clean so I can make you dirty again."

"Me, too." Tony soaped my asscrack, and slid a finger inside. I leaned over and bit his nipple. "Ouch, naughty boy." He buried his face in my neck. "I adore you."

"All this attention is making me dizzy."

"Get used to it. I feel twenty years younger; hell, my cock is hard again already."

"Who needs Viagra?"

"Not when I have a hot blond like you around. I'm sorry I've been neglecting you, baby. Forgive me?"

"Fuck me about five more times and you've got yourself a deal."

"I need it next. You ready for my ass?"

I shut off the water and grabbed a towel. "Race you to the bed." We were still dripping while we kissed. "You said you were going to lick me all over."

"And I meant it. But I want to start here." He pinched my butt. "Can you get up on your hands and knees for me?"

I almost had an orgasm right then. Tony knows getting rimmed is my personal favorite kink. My legs were quivering with excitement while I got into position. He spread me open, and teased my pucker with his tongue. I shoved a wad of sheet into my mouth to keep from screaming.

"Mmm, so good. You like that?"

"Fuuuuuuck," I mumbled around the wet fabric.

His tongue went deeper, darting in and out like a small velvet penis. He stopped, and sucked my balls while he massaged my taint with his thumbs.

"This is turning me on so much, I'm not going to make it."

I flipped over on my back. "Fuck me instead."

"It's your turn to fuck me, remember?"

"Where do you want it?"

Tony glanced around the room and grinned. "You know how you always wanted to do it in public, but I refused?"

"You want to go somewhere else?" Tony nodded. "Wow."

He kissed my nipples, then licked the tip of my dick. "Let's put some clothes on and take a stroll. Bring the lube."

We both put on pants and a shirt. I went barefoot; he had loafers on, no socks. We meandered around the hotel until we found an empty conference room.

"How about here?"

"Yeah, this is perfect. Fuck me on the table." I locked the door, but the chance of being caught was still there, and it caused us both to giggle like schoolboys. "Let's get naked."

We stripped, still laughing and blushing, both of our cocks ready to combust. Tony climbed on the table and pulled his legs back. He was spread open and vulnerable, panting with lust, his cock dripping onto his hairy stomach.

"I could come just from looking at you."

"Don't you dare. I want you inside. Get in here, fuck this ass." I rubbed lube into his hole and sucked his nipples while I teased a finger inside. "Mmm, fuck yeah, go in deep."

"I forgot how tight you are, it's been, what, five years?"

"Who cares how long it's been, fuck me." His voice was raspy and tight. I bit his nipple and he growled.

"My sexy grizzly bear is back. Fuck, I missed you. Growl for me some more." I added another finger and pushed deeper. He sucked in a breath. "There it is, your magic spot."

"Uhn. Holy shit, I think my cherry grew back. Damn."

"Shhh, relax, don't clench." I curled my fingers and rubbed. "Better?"

"I'm ready, give me your dick, stuff me."

"You're so hard again, it's amazing."

"I've never been so turned on, baby. Fuck me, quick, I want it."

I took my time as I slid my dick inside his tight ass. Enveloped in bliss, I felt all my heartache float away. Once I was buried deep, I leaned over and licked his tongue. It was like our first night together, all heat and raging hormones.

"How's my sweet virgin?"

"In heaven. I love you, Braiden, with all my soul."

His thighs gripped me tightly while I languidly thrust. He begged me to go harder, but I kept the pace slow and silky, to drive him crazy. It had been so long since I'd had the chance.

"What if some guy walked in right now?"

I put one of his legs over my shoulder and kissed the inside of his knee. "He would probably jack off while he watched. That would be hot."

"Braiden, I forgot how much I love this."

"Baby, you've made me fall in love with you all over again."

This was the Tony I missed, the one who was unafraid to love me, the one who smiled while he got fucked. He grinned and rubbed his own chest. I put my hands on top of his, and pounded his ass.

"You're fucking the cum out of me." Tony let out one more throaty growl, then cried out my name while he shot his load. "So good, so good, so good."

I knew he liked me to stop after he came, so I pulled out. "No, put it back, keep fucking me. I want you to come inside."

"Okay, baby, I want that, too."

Two more thrusts were all I needed. "Look at me, you're so sexy when you come."

I rested my head against his leg, mouth open, breathless; I licked his warm skin and fell into euphoric release. It was the most fulfilling orgasm I had ever had in my life.

"Tony, I love you so much, it scares me."

"Don't be scared, baby. I love you, too. We can rebuild this, right?"

"Yes, we can." I tried to pull out, but he crossed his ankles behind my back.

"Not yet. Can I just look at you? I want to memorize this moment. This is the day my life began again, I don't want to forget one second."

"If a man could die of happiness, I would croak right now." I kept my dick firmly wedged inside him while I licked the cum off his chest. "I missed the taste of you."

"Fuck, you're making me hard again."

The door rattled.

"Shit!" Tony hissed. I couldn't help but giggle.

"Get dressed, quick!" My semen gushed out of his ass and made a puddle on the table. "Whoops."

Tony laughed. "You filled me up good."

Someone knocked on the door. "Is anyone in there?"

"Yes, just a minute, please." I yanked on my clothes. The room smelled like sex, and we were both damp with sweat. I unlocked the door, and a young man with a name tag was standing just outside. "Sorry, we were thinking of holding a meeting here, and we needed to see if this conference room could fulfill our needs." I tried to sound professional.

The young man glanced back and forth between the two of us. "And did it?"

"Hell yeah, and then some," Tony said.

"What room are you staying in?"

"3067."

"I'll be sure to send up some champagne and a fruit platter, compliments of the hotel."

Tony blushed. "We'll clean up in here."

"No need, I'll send housekeeping. Enjoy the rest of your stay."

"Thank you."

I gave the clerk a quick kiss on the cheek, which caused him to blush. When the elevator doors closed behind us, Tony and I burst out laughing.

"Honest to fuck, that was the most exciting thing that's ever happened to me. You really surprised me, lover."

Tony grabbed my ass with both hands and stared into my eyes.

"Let's spend the rest of our lives surprising each other, Braiden."

"Sounds fantastic." Tony dropped to his knees.

"Marry me, Braiden."

"What?" My entire body spasmed in shock and awe.

"Marry me. We'll grow old together. What do you say?"

"I say, abso-fucking-lutely." I yanked him up by the front of his shirt and kissed him hard until the elevator doors opened. "Ready to get off?"

"Hell yeah." Tony pushed the button for the tenth floor and unzipped my pants.

A RIVIERA
WEDDING

Neil Plakcy

Aidan Greene lay back on the king-sized bed he shared with
his partner, Liam, illuminated by a shaft of late afternoon
sunlight. They had worked together at a job that morning,
watching the trophy wife and small children of a Russian
oligarch frolic on the pebbled beach at Nice. Since the wife was
so shapely and attractive, and preferred to sun herself topless, the
oligarch had specifically requested a pair of gay bodyguards.

It had been a hot, sweaty morning. Because he was so
muscular and physically imposing, Liam had been assigned the
more visible role, lying on a towel beside the family, wearing
only a pair of tight bikini briefs. Aidan, dressed in baggy shorts
and an extra-large T-shirt, had sat back at a table along the
Promenade des Anglais, with his gun in a quick-release holster
at his waist.

While Liam swam in the surf with the kids, then sunned
beside the wife, Aidan kept a lookout for predators. By the time
the family was ready to return to their hotel, he was drenched

in sweat and irritated. Liam escorted the clients back to their room, and Aidan returned to their apartment to shower and relax.

Now, naked, he sat back against the pillows and thought of Liam stepping out of the ocean with water cascading down his tanned, muscular arms, legs and chest. His two gold nipple rings glinted in the sunshine, and his hefty dick was outlined against white bikini briefs. It reminded Aidan of the first time he had seen his partner, years before, when Liam had been showering naked in the courtyard behind the Bar Mamounia in Tunis.

Back then, Aidan had watched him with a combination of lust and despair. Such a handsome, sexy guy, with an air of confidence. Aidan, who was on the run from a bad relationship, couldn't imagine having a chance with such a gorgeous man.

But then, after a wild ride through the Sahara, he and Liam had fallen in love, and Aidan had joined him as a bodyguard. Now, years later, they lived and worked together in Nice.

He reached down to touch his half-hard dick, running his index finger up its length, remembering how Liam had looked that morning, like a Greek god come to life. He closed his eyes and imagined Liam there beside him, how he'd turn to his partner and take one nipple ring between his teeth, and twist.

Liam would shiver and reach for Aidan's dick. Aidan stroked himself as he imagined that touch. He lay there in the shaft of sunlight gently fingering himself until his dick began to ooze precome.

"Getting started without me?"

Aidan opened his eyes to see Liam silhouetted in the doorway. His partner had an ability, cultivated by years as a U.S. Navy SEAL, to move quietly when he wanted to. It was almost creepy.

"Well, at least I waited for you to get here." He patted the bed beside him. Their little mixed-breed dog, Hayam, looked up from her place on the floor, then rested her head back down.

"I should take a shower."

"No, you shouldn't," Aidan said. "I love the way you smell when you've been out at the beach."

"Well, if you insist." Liam pulled off his T-shirt, revealing his narrow waist, awesome six-pack and beefy pecs. The gold nipple rings glinted dully in the light.

Aidan never tired of watching his partner strip. In the five years they had been together, Liam had put on a bit of weight around his hips, and his biceps were not as iron-hard as they'd once been. But even if that amazing body were to fall apart, Aidan knew he would still love the man inside.

Liam kicked off his leather sandals and stepped out of his baggy gray shorts. He usually wore a jockstrap, because he liked the way the cotton fabric cupped and protected his dick and balls, but that morning he'd skipped the jock in favor of the tiny bathing suit. As he skinned the white nylon down over his crotch, his half-hard dick popped out. He pushed the fabric down over his massive thighs and then let the suit fall to the floor.

Grinning, he struck a bodybuilder pose beside the bed—because he knew how much it teased and excited Aidan. As he did, he bounced his dick up and down a couple of times to stiffen it.

"Come here, you," Aidan said, clambering over the bed until his mouth was level with Liam's dick. Liam planted his legs firmly on the floor and Aidan reached out to cup Liam's balls. Then he moved in closer and took the mushroom head of Liam's beefy dick in his mouth.

Liam was a shower, not a grower; his dick was pretty much the same girth and length hard or soft. And either way, Aidan loved to take it in his mouth. Nestling his nose against Liam's pubic hair, he smelled the combination of sun, sand, salt water and tanning oil, along with their lavender soap and Liam's own unique musk.

Liam held his dick in one hand, and Aidan licked the fleshy pink mushroom cap. Then he stuck his tongue into the piss-slit as Liam jerked himself slowly, using Aidan's saliva as a lubricant. Aidan focused on sucking the head while Liam stroked the shaft. With his other hand, Liam leaned down and slapped Aidan's butt.

Aidan's body jerked but he kept on sucking. Liam spanked him, first one cheek then the other, and Aidan rubbed his stiff dick against the bed beneath him. He squirmed and writhed as the heat built up on his asscheeks and in his dick. His pulse accelerated as he felt Liam responding.

He closed his eyes and whimpered as the orgasm built in his gut, and Liam's body began to shake. Liam shot off in his mouth, one hand wrapped around his dick, the other on Aidan's head, holding him down. Aidan came onto the comforter, then stayed in place for a moment, savoring the feeling of Liam's dick in his mouth along with the exquisite pain of his sensitive dick against the cloth beneath him.

Liam took a deep breath and released his hold on Aidan, then stepped back. Aidan rolled onto his back, revealing the sticky mess beneath him. "You sure know how to put the 'come' in 'comforter,'" Liam said, laughing. "Now come on, let's get in the shower. We can't be late for this wedding."

"Not if we're the best men. You start the water, and I'll throw the comforter in the wash."

As Liam walked out of the bedroom, Aidan thought he detected more than the usual swagger in the sway of his partner's ass, and as much as he enjoyed seeing that ass naked, he was looking forward to seeing it encased in the handsome black tux he'd picked up the day before.

By the time he got to the bathroom Liam was already in the shower, and Aidan opened the glass door and stepped in beside him. It was a tight fit; Liam was six-four, Aidan a couple of inches shorter. Liam had always been brawny, and under his tutelage Aidan's muscles had grown as well. But the close quarters just made the maneuvering more fun, at least in Aidan's opinion.

Liam had already soaped himself up, and he pulled Aidan close, wrapping his arms around Aidan's back and leaning in for a deep kiss. They rubbed their bodies together, the lather transferring between them.

Aidan raised his arms over his head, and Liam rubbed soap into his pits, then lathered up his dick and balls. Aidan turned his back and bent forward a bit, and Liam inserted a soapy finger into Aidan's ass. He sighed with pleasure as Liam wiggled his finger around inside. "Gotta get you all cleaned up for your tuxedo," he said into Aidan's ear.

"Unless the tux has assless chaps with it, I don't think anyone else will know," Aidan said.

"I will," Liam said, leaning down to nibble at Aidan's earlobe.

Aidan turned back to face him, and they rinsed off in the shower spray. With his former partner, a bossy attorney he'd lived with in Philadelphia for ten years, Aidan could never have had so much fun in the shower. Blake wasn't a very sexual guy, and their encounters had been limited to mutual hand jobs and the occasional sixty-nine, always in their bed. With Liam, Aidan's sexual repertoire had expanded, and after five years living and working together, he still had an appetite for Liam's body that surpassed anything else he felt.

Would that ever change? he wondered, as he and Liam dried themselves with heavy Turkish towels. Would the magnetic attraction he felt for his partner lessen, the frequency of their encounters diminish? Could he ever imagine finding Liam's face, or the things he said, distasteful, the way he'd grown to dislike Blake in the years before Blake kicked him to the curb?

He hoped not. But there was no time for that kind of speculation; there was a wedding to start.

The wave of liberalization in feelings about gay people sweeping through the United States, from the demise of Don't Ask, Don't Tell to the cracks in the Defense of Marriage Act, had mattered little to Aidan and Liam, in their former home in Tunisia and now in Nice. Liam had left the Navy under DADT, and had no interest in returning to active duty. And for the two of them as expats, there was little motivation to marry even if they could.

Their friends Louis and Hassan, however, were in a different situation. Louis, an American by birth, was ostensibly a cultural attaché at the U.S. consulate in Nice, though his unspoken employer was the CIA. His longtime partner Hassan was an architect and Tunisian citizen. The two of them had moved from Tunis to Nice soon after Aidan and Liam had relocated there, when the State Department had loosened its policies on domestic partners.

But they'd still been in a kind of limbo. What if Louis were transferred somewhere else? Would Hassan be able to follow him? Once it became legal for them to marry in France, after a change in the law regarding foreign nationals, Louis had proposed to Hassan, and they had asked Aidan and Liam to be their groomsmen.

It was going to be a small ceremony at a restaurant in the small hilltop town of St. Paul de Vence, followed by another back in Washington DC, to be attended by Louis's family and his government friends. Then Louis could begin the paperwork to gain Hassan U.S. citizenship, securing their future together.

After they had accepted the invitation to participate in the wedding, Aidan had wondered if Liam would want to consider nuptials of their own. He'd known he was gay almost since puberty, so he'd never envisioned a wedding of his own, and he knew that Liam hadn't thought of one either. In fact, Liam disdained the concept, believing that gay divorce would soon follow gay marriage, only making work for attorneys.

But Aidan was a romantic, and the idea of pledging his troth to Liam, in front of family and friends, plucked at something inside his heart. As he and Liam put on their tuxedos he wondered if he'd ever be the one up at the altar, with Liam by his side.

Which altar, of course, could be a problem. Aidan had been raised in Reform Judaism, and though he hadn't been to a synagogue in a long time, he still felt culturally Jewish, lit Hanukkah candles and observed Rosh Hashanah and Yom Kippur. Liam had been educated by nuns and priests in Catholic schools. Though he wasn't observant in any way, Aidan knew that religious roots ran deep in his partner, particularly in the formation of his moral compass. So they'd probably have to compromise on a civil ceremony.

"Where are my dress shoes?" Liam asked.

"I had them polished," Aidan said. Neither of them dressed very formally, spending most of their work time in polo shirts, khaki slacks and deck shoes without socks. "They're on the floor in the closet."

He tied his own bow tie in the mirror, then turned to his partner. "You're going to have to lean down."

"Why couldn't we just get clip-on bow ties?" Liam grumbled, as he bowed his head.

"Louis is your best friend," Aidan said, as his fingers slipped through the intricate process. He'd often tied Blake's ties; Blake liked the look of hand-tied bows but didn't have the patience to learn himself. Aidan had taken care of that, along with everything else necessary to make Blake's life run smoothly—and look where it had gotten him.

"Louis is not my best friend," Liam muttered, his head down.

"If he's not, then who is?"

Liam lifted his head as Aidan stepped back. "You are."

"Fine. Then Louis is the best friend you have you don't sleep with." Aidan leaned back from Liam and surveyed his work, then tweaked one end of the bow. "You're good to go."

Aidan picked up the box of programs he'd had printed for the ceremony and followed Liam into their building's garage. Hassan's French was decent, but sometimes his accent interfered with what he wanted to say, and so Aidan had helped him with the details of the event—choosing the invitations, the restaurant and the menu, writing the program (in English and French), even joining him for a wedding cake tasting. Hassan, who had an impeccable sense of design (though a bit too Le Corbusier-modern for Aidan) had handled the decorations and the wedding outfits.

Liam drove them along the Promenade des Anglais until they turned inland at Cagnes-sur-Mer. It was a gorgeous day in late spring, with a scatter of thin cirrus clouds. Anemone, cowslip and wild jasmine bloomed along the roadside, and a field of lavender stretched toward the horizon. Aidan leaned his head out the window of the Jeep and Liam said, "You'll mess up your hair."

"Don't care," Aidan said, inhaling the country fragrance deeply.

The hilltop town, with its church tower the highest point, always took away his breath. It was so beautiful, especially with all the trees in full leaf. Liam pulled up into the garage at the entrance to the village, took his ticket and then pulled into a space. As he shut the car off, he reached out and took Aidan's hand. "Are you happy?"

"For Louis and Hassan? Of course." He opened the door. "Come on, let's go."

The restaurant was up a curved cobblestone street in an ancient two-story stone building, its doorstep so old that it had been smoothed by generations of village feet. There was also a series of stone steps that wound along the side of the building to the second-floor terrace, the railing hung with sweet-smelling honeysuckle vines.

They climbed to the terrace, which had views both toward the ocean and the foothills of the Alpes-Maritimes. The grooms stood beside the wrought-iron railings, their backs to the verdant hillside. Grapevines twined around a trellis above them. Louis, who'd be considered a bear by gay standards, filled out his pearl-gray tuxedo. He'd trimmed his dark beard into a devilish-looking goatee.

Slim-hipped Hassan was smooth-skinned, the color of a very light café crème, in a matching tux that he looked born to wear. After a round of hugs, kisses and handshakes, Louis asked Liam, "You have the rings?"

Liam turned to Aidan. "My PA has them."

"I don't care who has them as long as someone does."

Aidan pulled the two ring boxes from his jacket pocket. He opened the first and checked the inscription, then handed it to Liam. He kept the other for himself.

The minister was a pleasant middle-aged Englishwoman wearing white robes and a gold sash. She directed them to their places beneath the trellis, then walked through the ceremony quickly. Louis and Hassan retreated to the restaurant kitchen for a few moments together, and Liam and Aidan took their places: Liam at the door from the restaurant onto the terrace, Aidan at the head of the staircase. They handed out copies of the program and directed the guests to the folding chairs facing the hills, which Hassan had decorated with swags of green and white ribbons.

The church bell tolled five o'clock, and the guests took their seats. The minister walked out of the restaurant, and a slim woman with a portable keyboard began to play a tune Aidan recognized as Pachelbel's Canon in D. The restaurant door opened and Louis stepped out.

Aidan could tell he was nervous. He saw Liam put his arm around his friend's shoulder, and the two of them walked across the stone patio to the minister. When they arrived there, Liam removed his arm from Louis's shoulder and shook his hand. Then he stepped to the side.

Aidan turned to welcome Hassan from the staircase. He, too, looked nervous, but Aidan threaded his arm in Hassan's and walked him forward. When they reached the front, he let go of Hassan, kissed him on each cheek and then stepped to Liam's side.

The setting and the ceremony were so incredibly romantic that Aidan couldn't stop smiling. The minister welcomed everyone and then turned to Aidan, who stepped forward and pulled a folded piece of paper from his pocket. Using his best "teacher voice," he read the 98th psalm, which ended with "Let the sea roar, and all that fills it; the world and those who live in it. Let the floods clap their hands; let the hills sing together for joy at the presence of the Lord, for he is coming to judge the earth. He will judge the world with righteousness, and the peoples with equity."

He had scoured the Bible and a dozen or more gay wedding websites, looking for a blessing that might be appropriate, and he loved the reference to sea and hills, and the reference to righteousness and equity.

There was an appreciative murmur from the crowd when Aidan finished. He folded the paper again and stepped back to Liam's side.

The minister thanked him and then turned to Louis. "Your vows?" she asked him.

Louis held his hands out to Hassan, who took them. "Hassan, I have loved you since the first time I saw you. If you will do me the great honor of becoming my husband I promise to love you and care for you, wherever our lives take us, in sickness and in health, in good fortune and ill." His voice quavered, and he looked on the verge of tears. Aidan could see him take a deep breath when he finished.

The minister turned to Hassan and smiled.

"Louis, when I felt darkness all around me, you brought me light." His English was heavily accented, and his voice quavered as much as Louis's. Aidan loved the way he elongated the s at the end of Louis's name.

"You have been the steadying force in my life, and your love has helped me become the man I have always wanted to be. I promise to stand by your side, to hold you and love you and bring you as much joy as you have brought me."

Aidan fished in his pants pocket for a tissue and dabbed at his eyes. Then he turned to Liam and smiled, squeezing his hand. Liam smiled back at him.

Louis and Hassan turned to face the minister. She said, "In

light of the vows you have made, in the sight of the company here assembled to witness them, and in accordance with the laws of France, I hereby proclaim you married partners." She turned to the audience. "Please join me in a blessing of this union. From the first book of Samuel: 'Jonathan became one in spirit with David, and he loved him as himself. And Jonathan made a covenant with David because he loved him as himself.' Let us pray that Louis and Hassan shall be as David and Jonathan, one in sprit and one in love. And then let us say, 'Amen.'"

The crowd joined her. Then she turned to Louis and Hassan. "As is the custom around the world, please seal your union with a kiss."

Louis and Hassan leaned toward each other. Then Louis put his hand behind Hassan's head and dipped him low, kissing him deeply, and the audience applauded. Everyone stood, and while a server passed around flutes of champagne, others moved the chairs around tables and brought out platters for a buffet. It was all lovely, and Hassan and Louis couldn't stop holding hands and smiling.

By the time the sun finally set over the hills, only Aidan and Liam were left at the restaurant with their friends. "I can't thank you enough for everything," Louis said. "Without Aidan's help planning we might have had a disaster."

"Is this a trial run for your own wedding?" Hassan asked mischievously.

"You forget, we both have U.S. citizenship," Liam said. "So it's not necessary for us."

"The citizenship issue isn't the reason we got married," Louis said, with a twang of tension in his voice. "It's icing on the cake, sure. But the real reason is that Hassan and I love each other, and we want to share that with our friends and families."

Aidan knew that Hassan's family disapproved of his sexuality, and none of them had flown to France for the ceremony. But he also knew that many gay men had families of choice rather than birth, and he was happy to be part of their circle.

"And I love you, too, *habibi*," Hassan said, using the Arabic for sweetheart. They hung behind to settle the bill with the restaurant, and Aidan and Liam walked back down the hill to the garage.

Aidan waited until they were in the car to say anything. "That was rude, you know," he said as Liam drove through the gathering darkness. "To assume that they got married just so Hassan could get citizenship."

"It's the truth, isn't it? They wouldn't have bothered with a stupid ceremony otherwise."

"I thought it was romantic," Aidan said. "Not stupid at all." He turned toward the window so that Liam wouldn't see the tear that had formed in the corner of his eye.

"You know how I feel," Liam said. "Marriage is for straight people. We don't need a piece of paper or overpriced jewelry to justify our love."

Liam had never been shy about voicing his opinion about gay marriage. He cited studies that indicated men were biologically driven to spread their seed to multiple partners, to perpetuate their DNA. When Aidan countered, asking then for the biological basis of homosexuality, Liam said that it was Mother Nature's way of birth control.

The topic infuriated Aidan, who believed in romance, in monogamy and the chance to have a big party, so he usually avoided it. But at the wedding, when he'd tried in his mind's eye to see himself and Liam standing there together, he had realized that it was never going to happen. There were too many obstacles, from their different religious backgrounds to Liam's staunch opposition.

That, even more than the romantic sight of Louis and Hassan pledging to each other, was what had made him cry at the ceremony. He knew it was childish, like throwing a tantrum after seeing a toy he wanted but couldn't have. And the logical part of his brain said that if what he really wanted was to get married, then he had to find a man who would marry him. If Liam wasn't that man...

And yet, Aidan felt more fully himself with Liam than ever before, with or without a partner. Liam challenged him to grow in ways that Aidan knew he needed to. He showed Aidan his love every day, from the bedroom to the job to the briefest of glances. He was fiercely protective of Aidan, and always grateful for the way Aidan had rescued him from a self-imposed solitude.

Where was the solution? Neither of them spoke for the rest of the ride home. Aidan took Hayam out for her late night walk, and when he returned, Liam was propped up in bed with the top sheet pulled up to his waist, his reading glasses on and a personal protection journal in his hands. Aidan remembered that the comforter was in the washer and needed to be dried; would they be able to sleep without it?

He was thinking of that as he walked to the closet and began taking off his dress shoes. Behind him, he heard Liam put the glasses and the magazine on the bedside table. "You know that I love you," Liam said.

"Of course," Aidan said, as he hung up the tuxedo jacket. He would return the rented suits the next day. "And I love you."

"Then why isn't that enough? Why can't we make our own private commitment to each other and be done?"

Aidan stepped out of his slacks and hung them neatly. He

turned back to Liam in his tuxedo shirt, still held together by fake mother-of-pearl studs.

"I don't know, Liam." Aidan kept his head down and began trying to undo the studs, but his hands wouldn't work.

Liam stood up. He was naked, and his dick was curled up, resting in the nest of his pubic hair. He reached over and gently began undoing the studs from the shirt. "Is it that important to you?"

Aidan looked up. "I thought that Blake and I would be together forever," he said. "But all it took to destroy our relationship was one bad day. He told me to get out, I packed a bag and I was on a plane that night."

Liam slipped the shirt from Aidan's shoulders and tossed it into the laundry hamper. "I won't ever do that to you," he said softly. "I'm not Blake Chennault, and you don't need a piece of paper to hold onto me."

He took Aidan's face in his hands. "Do you know that every morning I thank God for Blake?"

Aidan looked in his brown eyes, which seemed so deep and loving. "Blake? Why would you thank God for him?"

"Because he sent you to me," Liam said. "If he hadn't been such a jerk, you might still be in Philadelphia with him, instead of here with me."

Aidan leaned forward and kissed him, blinking back tears. His stomach churned with emotion and he wrapped his arms around his partner's smooth back. Liam pulled back and smoothed a lock of hair from Aidan's forehead. Then he stepped back, and lowered himself to one knee.

He reached for Aidan's hand. "Aidan Greene, will you marry me?"

It was so not what Aidan was expecting that he stood there openmouthed. He looked down and saw Liam's dick unfurling and suddenly the churning feeling in his stomach was gone, replaced by a lightness.

"I want nothing more than to spend the rest of my life beside you." Aidan reached down for Liam's hands and tugged him upward.

As Liam stood, Aidan continued. "I appreciate that you are willing to marry me because it's important to me, even though it's not something you'd ordinarily do." He leaned up and kissed Liam's lips lightly. "But if we marry someday, it will be because we both want to, for ourselves as well as for each other."

"Is that a no?" Liam asked.

Aidan shook his head. His heart was racing and his dick was stiff, but he'd never been more sure of something. "Consider it a kind of promissory note. When the time is right, I'll say yes."

"I'll hold you to that," Liam said.

Aidan smiled wickedly. "You know, a note like that is usually accompanied by a good faith deposit." He stepped back and dropped his shorts, his stiff dick bouncing against his abdomen. Liam was hard by then, too. Aidan sat on the bed, then leaned back against the pillows and raised his legs. "First National Bank of Aidan, now open for deposits."

Liam laughed. "You are crazy, but in a good way. I'll be right back."

He returned from the bathroom a moment later holding a bottle of lubricant. They had long since stopped using condoms, after they were confident they were healthy and committed to monogamy.

Liam squeezed a dollop out and stroked his dick, smiling lasciviously at Aidan. Aidan felt as horny as he'd ever been, desperate to feel his lover inside him. He pulled apart his asscheeks and Liam stuck his gooey index finger inside him.

Aidan groaned with pleasure as the cold lube warmed

inside him, and Liam's long, rough finger snaked its way up his channel. "Oh god," he groaned.

Liam looked up at him. "You can just call me Liam."

Aidan swatted him on the shoulder. "Focus, baby. I want you in me."

"All things come to he who waits," Liam said, but he pulled his finger out and positioned his dick at Aidan's hole.

His powerful muscular thighs gave him incredible control when it came to ass-fucking. He moved into Aidan, centimeter by centimeter, and Aidan thought he couldn't take any more of Liam's beefy dick. And then he took more, until the head of Liam's dick was nosing against Aidan's prostate. Then Liam pulled back ever so slowly.

Aidan felt his emptiness reverberate through him, until Liam entered him again, this time moving a bit more quickly, gradually building his rhythm so that every thrust rubbed against Aidan's channel and banged into his prostate, and he was squirming on the bed, whimpering and moaning. His dick was so hard it hurt, and precome streamed down from the head, but he didn't touch himself. Liam had such awesome control of his body that he was able to sense when his orgasm was rising and then pull back, slow down until the impulse passed and then begin again.

Aidan didn't know which he wanted more, to ejaculate himself, or to feel Liam shoot off in his ass. Finally, though, he could feel Liam give in to his impulse, and Liam wrapped his rough palm around Aidan's dick and jerked him just a couple of strokes. "Come on, baby, come for me," Liam said. "Drive me over the edge."

Aidan was only too happy to oblige. He shot off in Liam's fist and a moment later felt Liam slam into his ass and the hot spurt of come inside him. Liam stayed inside him until his dick had stopped pulsing, and then he pulled out carefully and flopped over onto his back.

"That was amazing," he said.

"I guess you should propose every day," Aidan said.

Liam laughed. "If that's what it takes to make you happy, sweetheart, consider it done."

Aidan curled against Liam, his head resting on his partner's chest, and Liam reached his arm around Aidan's shoulders. Aidan knew that he ought to get up, clean up, put the comforter in the dryer, take the dog out for her late-night walk—but for that moment, all he wanted to do was lie in the arms of the man who loved him, and whom he loved.

HOMECOMING

Justin Josh

The look on Scott's face was thinly disguised disappointment mixed with disgust. Perfect, I thought. The apartment was a total mess. I was dirty, unshaven (which Scott hated), and best of all, I wore a fat-suit hidden beneath a full-length cotton robe. I looked terrible.

Scott stood in the doorway, shocked. He looked gorgeous, decked out in his spotless uniform with its gleaming gold buttons. He knew how much I loved the way he looked in full uniform. With his puppy-dog brown eyes framed with those thick eyebrows, he was irresistible.

I could only imagine what he must be thinking, coming home from Afghanistan after six months only to find his boyfriend dressed in a bathrobe before dinner and looking like he had gained a hundred pounds.

Scott loved practical jokes and this was big. Cruel, perhaps, but he deserved this for all the surprises he had pulled on me, and for telling me before he left that I was getting chubby, and most of all for teasing me about all the beautiful muscular men he was working with while in the Army.

"Welcome home," I said, hugging him. I could barely keep from laughing as he recoiled. "Sorry about the mess." I waved at the carefully staged destruction of our small apartment. Dirty dishes and old food covered the tables and countertops. Soiled clothes were strewn across the couch and floor.

To his credit, Scott gulped, smiled weakly and kissed me. He began to fondle my body, clearly surprised at how much weight I had gained. I pulled away, feigning embarrassment.

"Later," I said. "You just got home."

Scott looked almost like he was going to cry. Had I gone too far?

"I can't believe you didn't clean up," he said. "You knew I was coming."

"I'm sorry," I said. "I cooked for us. I made your favorite: lasagna and garlic bread. You go upstairs, take a shower and change into something more comfortable. Give me an hour and I'll get everything ready."

"Okay," he said, leaning forward to kiss me again.

He kissed me and grabbed my butt. Again, he looked at me strangely.

"You gained weight," he said, neutrally.

I put on my best guilty face. "I'm sorry. I'll lose it, I promise."

"I've missed you, Todd," he said.

"Me too."

He nodded, turned and walked upstairs.

I nearly laughed out loud. Poor Scott! He had no idea that beneath my fat-suit was my new finely sculpted muscular body. He was right. I had been getting chubby. So right after he left, I began working out on a daily basis. Not only did I lose my chubbiness, my muscles filled out quite nicely. I even had an actual six-pack. Scott was going to be so surprised.

As I heard him step into the shower, I went into a tornado of activity. Most of the mess was fake, so I quickly turned the living room into a place of beauty. I turned on some soft music, lit some candles and sage incense and moved to the kitchen.

In moments, I had the dishes in the dishwasher, the home-made lasagna in the oven and a garden salad chilling in the refrigerator.

I set the table with the fine dishes, cloth napkins and a chilled bottle of red wine.

Then I popped into the downstairs bathroom, took off the fat-suit, and cleaned up.

I couldn't wait for Scott to see my new body. I wasn't sure how much longer I could hide it from him. At least until after dinner, I told myself. I would wear the fat-suit and robe for a little while longer. But beneath them I put on my brand new piece of exotic underwear.

Scott had an underwear fetish and he loved to see me in various types of thongs and under gear. Today I would wear a mankini, a skimpy nylon thong with long spaghetti straps that went over my shoulders. I looked stunning in it, and I knew it would drive Scott wild.

I was back in the kitchen, fully wrapped up in my robe and fat-suit and working on the garlic bread when Scott came down.

Gone was all trace of disappointment. He looked around at the clean apartment, at my freshly scrubbed face and hair, and he smiled widely, giving me another kiss and hug. He was dressed in a loose white T-shirt and tight cotton sweatpants that showed off his manly bulge.

I longed to play with it, but I knew that once we started,

we wouldn't stop. So I restrained myself and continued to fix dinner.

"Still wearing the robe," he said.

"I'm just embarrassed," I said. "I've gained so much weight."

"It's all right," Scott said. "I don't mind, really."

It was obvious that he did, but it was awesome of him to say that he didn't. I nearly whipped off my clothes right there.

Soon, I chanted to myself. *Soon.*

We ate dinner and Scott talked about his experiences in the Army. Things were different with the abolition of Don't Ask, Don't Tell. A few times Scott had come close to being discovered and kicked out. Now we no longer had to worry about that.

"I was surprised," said Scott, between bites. "The guys were really great about it. There was this one guy, he was kind of effeminate. There was no use for Don't Ask, Don't Tell. With that guy, it was: Don't Ask, It's Obvious!"

"Did anybody come on to you?"

Scott laughed. "Don't worry, Todd. No need to be jealous. Yes, they did, but I just showed them a photo of you, and once they saw how handsome you are, they backed off." He kissed me gently. "This lasagna is fantastic."

I smiled. Scott always knew exactly what to say. The photo I had given him was slightly racy. It showed me grinning at him with my head turned while I stood naked in the shower, my bare-naked ass in full view. I thought of all the guys he had shown that to and felt a thrill race through my body.

I got up to do the dishes.

"Oh, hell no!" Scott said, jumping up. "Let me do them for you."

He whipped off his shirt and revealed his muscular hairy chest, posing briefly for me.

I laughed. "You're just trying to seduce me," I accused him.

"Is it working?" he asked.

"It might be," I said teasingly.

"All right then. Will you hand me those?" He stood before the sink and pointed to the dishes on the table.

I scooped them up and dropped them in the sink. He began to rinse them and put them in the dishwasher, while I took a dishcloth and wiped the table.

In moments we were finished.

We moved to the living room with our glasses of wine and settled on the couch.

It was time for the big reveal.

"I haven't been entirely honest with you," I told Scott.

"What do you mean?" He looked truly alarmed. Honesty had always been paramount in our relationship.

"It's nothing bad," I said, smiling. "In fact, I think you might like it."

"Really?" he said, leaning back and showing off his marvelous abs. He crossed his arms behind his neck, making his biceps bulge enticingly. I wanted to pounce on him right then and there. "I'm listening."

"Maybe it's better if I just show you."

"Show me?" His eyebrows rose in surprise. "Now you really got me curious. Okay."

"Let me just go upstairs and get it," I said.

"You bought something?" he asked. He knew how frugal I was.

"You might say that."

He laughed. "Okay, go on, then. Show me. I don't know what you're up to, but hurry back. I'm getting horny."

I couldn't help it. I giggled mischievously. This was going to be amazing.

I dashed upstairs, and removed the fat-suit. Then I put the robe back on and walked back downstairs.

Scott watched as I approached. I kept my hands behind my back, pretending to hide something.

With great fanfare I stood before him while he sat on the couch, and I removed my hands from behind my back and held them out in front of him.

He looked at my empty hands in confusion.

I smiled and very slowly, I began to undo my robe. First I untied the waist-strap and let it hang loose.

Then I played with the collar, loosening it slowly. First I lifted one side, and then the other. Finally I stepped out of my robe and stood before him wearing nothing but the little white mankini, which due to my excitement, could barely contain me.

My body was freshly cleaned and shaved and oiled. My muscles bulged in all the right places as I began doing various poses for my man.

Scott howled with shock. His eyes bulged out and his face showed utter astonishment. He began smiling widely, his mouth open and his tongue hanging out.

"Todd! I don't believe it! You look incredible!"

I couldn't take it any longer. I lunged forward and wrapped my nearly naked body around him. I could feel his whole body shudder with pleasure as I began to kiss his lips and neck. I worked my way down to his nipples and took first one and then the other into my mouth.

He arched his back and groaned. I knew exactly what he liked and was able to render him completely helpless. He began to hyperventilate as I kissed his armpits.

At the same time, he couldn't keep his hands off me. He kept fondling my shoulders and chest, amazed at the transformation. I shuddered under his touch.

"Man, Todd," he whispered into my ear. "You are such a stud. Now get up and take off that thing. Don't get me wrong. I think you look great in it, but right now I want you buck naked."

"Yes, sir," I said jokingly. I stood up and removed the mankini and gave him a full salute, in more than one way.

Scott quickly removed his sweatpants and sat down naked on the couch, his cock resting hard against his abdomen. He looked like a Greek god.

Scott grabbed me roughly, pulled me facedown across his lap and began playing with my ass, spanking it and running his fingers up and down my crack. His touch was magical, sending pulses of pleasure through my body like lightning.

He knew that a nibble to my earlobe or a caress against my naked buttcheek was enough to paralyze me with pleasure. He knew that with his grip around the base of my shaft, I was a puppet in his hands.

He took complete advantage of his knowledge, causing me so much pleasure I had to beg him for reprieve. Finally, he relented.

Now it was time for revenge! I knew him just as well as he knew me. More than anything, Scott loved a great blow job.

And I had been fascinated with his cock from first sight. The size of a flashlight, it stuck out straight at me now, calling for my lips.

"Sit down," I told Scott. "Spread your legs and put your hands behind your neck."

Scott hesitated. We were both extremely sensitive after being apart from each other for so long. It was hard for him to sit still while I knelt down before him.

I tortured him mercilessly by kissing first his nipples and then working my way down his chest to his heaving abs.

While I ran my fingers lightly over his chest, I moved lower, kissing him in his furry triangle of pubic hair, making him moan.

Then I moved farther down and kissed his inner thighs. He immediately tried to close his legs, but I held them open and kissed him harder.

He began to shudder and groan.

At that moment, I took his balls into my mouth, and he howled with pleasure. He immediately started dripping like a faucet. "Please!" he said. "Mercy! Please!"

He wanted me to take him. Not yet, chump! I worked his balls for several more minutes, bringing poor Scott to a state of almost total submission. Only then did I release him and move toward the goal.

I began to kiss and lick his shaft on the underside, back and forth several times until Scott couldn't take it any longer. He grabbed my head and forced me to swallow him.

I took all of him in willingly, while he guided my head back and forth and made those masculine grunting noises that only I could make him do.

I worked him expertly, bringing him to the brink of climax, but never letting him quite reach it. I played him like a musical instrument, until finally he was pleading for me to stop.

"Please," he begged. "Either stop or let me cum. I can't take it anymore."

"Okay," I said, guiltily. "I'm sorry. You know how much I enjoy torturing you. It's just so good to have you back."

"You too," he said. "And you look great. I'm so proud of you." He began grabbing my ass. "Do you want to go to the bedroom?"

He didn't have to ask me twice. I raced up there with Scott hot on my heels, grabbing my naked butt the whole way.

We jumped into bed and made love for the next three hours, finally resting together in each other's arms. We talked about how completely I had fooled him, and how happy he was with my new body. He vowed to get me back for the joke I had pulled on him. We talked about how much we had missed each other, and how awful it would be when he had to go away again. Scott had only two more years of service before he had the option to leave with a full education in electronic engineering.

He had always told me that he planned on leaving the Army so we could spend more time together. Now, however, as we began to talk about the future, he began to get evasive. He wouldn't tell me how long we had together until he had to leave next.

"You don't know your next assignment yet?"

"No, I know," he said. "I just don't want to tell you right now. Please can't we talk about this tomorrow?"

"I don't know. Will you be here?"

"Stop it," he said. "Of course I will."

"Why won't you tell me? How long do we have? Please tell me it's more than one day."

He laughed. "Don't worry; it's more than a day."

"Oh, two then? Three? I just don't understand why you won't tell me."

He sighed. "Fine, I'll tell you. But you're not going to like it."

I looked at him sadly. I just knew it. He was going away again.

"Three days," he said.

I began crying.

Scott pulled me into his arms. Even though it wasn't his fault, he looked incredibly guilty. "I'm sorry," he said. "I didn't mean to make you cry."

"I just don't want you to go," I said. "I miss you so much when you're gone."

"Me too," he said, tears starting to form in his eyes. He coughed and brushed them away. "Stop it. You're making us both sad."

"I'm sorry," I said. "I'll be good. We'll just have to make do with the time we have."

"Don't worry," he said. "You're going to love it."

As I fell asleep in his arms, I wondered about what he said. What did he mean, I was going to love it? Love what? Did he have something planned?

I woke up the next morning to find the bed empty and the smell of fresh coffee and eggs wafting into the room.

Scott always was an early riser. If I was correct, he would be freshly showered and dressed in nothing but an apron while he fixed breakfast. It was already nine thirty. He had let me sleep late.

I giggled. I was so happy to have him back, even if only for a few days. I showered quickly so that I wouldn't waste a moment of being with him.

I dressed up in my sexiest jeans and shirt and went to the kitchen.

There Scott stood, naked except for the apron, with a guilty grin.

He looked at my clothes. We both knew that I would be naked shortly after breakfast. But meanwhile, I intended to look my best.

We ate and talked about what we would do that day, besides have sex.

That's when I realized that Scott was flashing me his "I have a secret" smile.

"Okay," I said. "What are you hiding?"

"What are you talking about?" he asked innocently, sipping his coffee too loudly and letting his gaze wander around. He was a terrible liar. I could read him like my favorite book.

"Don't even bother trying to deny it. I can tell you're up to something. You're trying to get me back for my joke, aren't you? What is it?"

He shook his head and gave me the stare-down. "Not at all," he said. "You've got it all wrong." He quickly looked away. Damn those puppy-dog eyes! They almost caused me to lose my train of thought.

"What is it, then? I know you're hiding something."

"Fine," he said, still smiling. "I haven't been entirely honest with you either."

"What?" I said. I could tell by his expression that he was suddenly very excited and nervous about something.

"I've planned a big surprise for you," he said.

"What?" I asked. I stood up and began putting the dishes in the sink and refreshing our coffee cups. I began cleaning while he sat at the table and drank his coffee.

He laughed. "Maybe it's better if I just show you."

I nearly dropped the dishes. I turned and looked at him, while he stood.

"I'll be right back," he said, and he dashed up the stairs.

I continued cleaning the kitchen as quietly as I could, listening. I heard him shuffling around upstairs. What was he doing? And what was taking him so long?

Finally I heard him walk out of the room to the top of the stairs.

"Close your eyes!" he shouted.

"What? Why?" My heart beat wildly.

"Just do it! Or I'm not coming down."

"Fine," I said. I closed my eyes. What was he up to? After

what I had done to him, I was both terrified and excited. He probably had something really sexy planned. But what?

"Are your eyes closed?"

"Yes," I said.

I heard him walk down the stairs. I could almost feel him staring at me, checking to make sure I wasn't looking.

I stood before the kitchen sink, my hands on the counter to steady myself, waiting.

I heard him approach behind me.

"Turn around and open your eyes," he said.

I obeyed and didn't see him. Then I looked down in shock.

Scott was on his knees. He was dressed in a tuxedo and looked more beautiful than I had ever seen him before.

Only then did I realize he held something in his hand: a small box.

He opened it. Inside was a bright gleaming gold band. I gasped.

"Oh my god."

"I told you I had a surprise."

"Yes!" I screamed. "Yes!"

He laughed. "You didn't even let me ask!"

"Go ahead," I said, jumping up and down.

Scott proceeded to give a very eloquent and traditional proposal, asking for my hand in marriage. We had talked about marrying many times, but until recently, the laws had not allowed it. I had been thinking about asking Scott, but now he'd beat me to it. And I couldn't have been happier.

"Yes!" I screamed again, and trembled as he put on my ring.

I planted a huge kiss on him and apologized for crying.

"Okay," he said, pointing to a huge box on the table. I hadn't even noticed it was there. "Get dressed," he said.

"What is that?"

"It's your tuxedo. We're getting married today. All our friends and family are waiting. Your parents, mine, all our cousins, aunts, uncles...everybody."

I looked at him in shock.

"Oh, and one more thing," he said. "I've been honorably discharged. I finished my education, so now I'm all yours."

"You're joking."

He shook his head and grinned wickedly at me. "I told you I would get you back."

I wasn't sure whether to hit him or kiss him. So I did both. I grabbed the box. "This isn't over," I warned him, and I dashed upstairs to prepare for the happiest day of my life.

LATE START

Heidi Champa

I gave myself a once-over in the full-length mirror and smoothed my lapels. God, I hated wearing suits. And whoever decided it was a good idea to keep wearing ties after the invention of the button needed to be shot. But they were a hazard of the job. I picked up my watch and fixed the clasp into place, glancing down at the time before I picked up my briefcase and headed for the front door. Until I was stopped dead in my tracks. By Ben.

"What are you doing out of bed?"

He looked at me with tired eyes. "I made you coffee."

"I can see that." I could also see that he was sitting naked on the couch, pretending it was the most normal thing in the world, even though it was anything but common. When I first woke up, I tried to be quiet so as not to disturb him. Ben wasn't much of an early riser. When I tiptoed into the bathroom to shower, he was tucked up under the covers, looking adorable. Somewhere in the time it took me to get dressed and ready to leave for my train out of town, he'd woken up. The smell of fresh-ground beans filled the room and I was torn between getting myself a cup and staring at Ben's body a little more. He smirked as he sipped from his mug, crossing his ankles on the coffee table. The morning paper was strewn all over the place, our cat Sadie nestled in the pages of the sports section.

"Why don't you join me, Cam?"

"Because I have a train to catch. You know that."

"Not for a little while yet. You have time for one cup, don't you? It's barely eight."

He gave a coy smile and brought his mug to his lips, staring at me until I relented.

"Fine, I'll have a cup. But then I really have to go."

"Whatever you say, Cam."

I looked over at him and saw that his face had fallen, his eyes focused on the mug cradled in his hands.

"Don't pout, baby. I'll be back before you know it."

I walked to the kitchen and filled my own cup with steaming goodness and took a few steps toward the couch. Ben ran a lazy hand down his chest and I stopped in my tracks.

"Why are you leaving so early anyway? You don't have to be in DC until tonight."

"I told you, Jeffrey from the home office wants to have lunch and discuss the meeting tonight. We have to pregame, as he calls it."

He rolled his eyes, tapping his fingers against his white porcelain mug.

"Oh, right. Sounds boring. That Jeffrey uses way too many sports metaphors for someone who's never played a sport."

I smiled for a moment, trying not to get sidetracked by his attempts to bait me into another discussion about my job.

"Everything I do sounds boring to you, Ben. But we all can't be painters."

"You only say that because you're terrible at art, Cam."

"True enough."

He drank the rest of his coffee and dropped the cup on the table. This time, as he slouched back, he left his legs gloriously open. He wrapped his fist around his dick and stroked slowly up and down.

"You should stay for a little while longer at least. Spend some time with your husband. We're still supposed to be in the honeymoon phase after all."

"We've been together too long to still be in the honeymoon phase. We did all that seven years ago."

He chuckled for a moment, before letting out a rattling cough, the remnants of a cold he'd been battling the week before. I was just about to ask him how he was feeling, but he didn't give me the chance, his response dripping with sarcasm.

"God, you're such a romantic, Cam. I don't know how I'm supposed to stand it."

"You know what I mean. It's not my fault we couldn't get married until a few months ago."

"That doesn't mean we can't act like newlyweds. Because, you know, sweetie, we actually are."

"I promise when I get back, we'll do something."

"We could do something right now."

He looked at me expectantly and it took everything I had to get the next words out. "I'm sorry, I really have to go."

Ben stared at me, his hand still moving around his cock, a little moan slipping past his lips before he spoke.

"Killjoy."

I sipped my coffee and glanced at my watch. I really did have to leave. Technically, I should have already been on my way to the train station. It was so typical of Ben to try and distract me on a day like today. There he sat, on our giant sofa, bathed in the morning sun, every curtain in the loft wide open. Light bounced off the whitewashed brick walls, making everything glow. In the middle of it all was Ben, without a care in the world, his dark brown hair a mess, the glint in his eye making me reconsider my plans. For a moment, at least. The sky was the most gorgeous blue and I could hear the noise of the city getting louder as more and more people flooded onto the streets to start their day. Just like I was supposed to be doing. I repeated my words, but I said them more for me than for him.

"I really have to go, Ben."

He sighed and ran his free hand up and down his thigh.

"So you said. Then go. Call me when you get to our nation's capital."

His words were flat, but I barely heard them. Mostly because Ben was making it hard for me to focus on anything but his hard dick. I looked at my watch, but I barely even saw the numbers. I knew I should just go. Then, Ben opened his mouth again.

"I'll miss you, baby."

His voice came out a bit husky, a trick he used when he wanted to get his way. The sound of it always drove me crazy, even after all these years. Which he knew, of course. He stretched an arm up into the air, his head coming to rest against the back of the couch. While I kept watching him, I found myself setting down my briefcase and loosening the knot on my tie. Ben smiled as I toed off my shoes on my way to the couch, careful to lay my suit jacket over the back of his favorite chair. I stood right in front of him and looked down at him, his hand still moving slowly up and down his dick.

"I thought you had to go, Cam. I mean, you have that lunch date and all."

I smiled at his sarcasm, but otherwise ignored it.

"I do have to go. But, there's something I want to do first."

I leaned down and gave him a kiss, his lips still tasting of the coffee he'd just finished. Ben scooted forward on the couch and grabbed me by the belt, undoing the buckle with quick hands. The wool pants slid down my legs to the floor and I felt the tickle of Ben's fingertips sliding under the waistband of my boxers. I put my hands to his to stop him, to get my trip back on track. Someone had to be practical, after all.

But, then I looked down into his gorgeous heavy-lidded eyes. My last bit of resolve, the last practical thought in my head disappeared.

"What's wrong, Cam?"

I shook my head and ran my hand through his hair, the morning sun dancing off the strands. Damn, he was so cute.

"Nothing."

As the word came out of my mouth, I undid the strap of my watch and dropped it to the table. At that moment, it really didn't matter what time it was.

Ben looked up at me with a smile and started lowering my boxers before I could protest again. My cock sprung free, brushing against the week's worth of stubble covering his face. His eyes fluttered closed as his lips closed around me. In that moment, everything stopped. Everything except the exquisite sweep of his tongue along my shaft. I gave up on the rest of the buttons and yanked my dress shirt and the white tee underneath it over my head, tossing them aside. Wrinkles were suddenly the least of my worries. My fingers tightened in his hair as he took me deep and I moaned out my words.

"Fuck, Ben. That feels so good."

He looked up at me and grasped the base of my dick, his tongue swirling around the head until my knees buckled. It only took a small tug at my wrist to pull me down to the couch next to him and I took Ben's face in my hands, giving him a kiss. He eased back and slipped my glasses from my face, placing them gently on the table. Everything went hazy and fuzzy around the edges. I hated not being able see him properly, but I'd busted too many pairs over the years to keep them on when we had sex.

Ben shoved me onto my back and nestled between my legs, my cock back in his mouth before I could say a word. The sun streaked across his back and I couldn't resist running my hands over his soft, warm skin. When I felt his lips close around one of my balls, I cried out, the sound echoing off the walls. The sound made Sadie run under the chair, kicking up pieces of newsprint as she scampered away. From across the room, I heard my cell phone ring from the confines of my briefcase. Ben stopped and looked up at me, his hand still jerking my cock.

"You're not going to get that are you?"

I grinned, thinking back to the one time I'd made that mistake, years before.

"No, I've learned my lesson. Don't worry."

He slithered up my body and kissed me, our tongues tangling as the electronic noise finally stopped. No doubt it was Jeffrey checking to make sure I made it onto the train, which was probably pulling out of the station without me at that very moment. But I couldn't care.

"I should hope so. After the Valentine's Day debacle."

"God, I mess up one time. You remember everything, don't you Ben?"

"Yup, including how much you like this."

His mouth went to my neck and I felt his teeth sink into my skin, not enough to really hurt, but enough to make my back arch off the couch. Ben kissed his way down until I felt his teeth close around my nipple, a gasp coming out of my mouth before I could stop it.

"Fuck."

I hissed out the word, my hands twining roughly through Ben's hair. Guiding him back to my cock, I watched through blurry eyes as he took it back in his mouth. Even with my terrible vision, the sight of my dick disappearing down his throat made my toes curl against the couch cushion. As much as I wanted to let him go on forever teasing me, I reluctantly pulled back.

"What's wrong, Cam?"

"Nothing."

"Then why did you stop me?"

"I think you know why."

Ben smirked, giving the head of my cock a kiss before crawling over me until his knees were on either side of my chest. I looked up at him for a moment, his hand stroking his dick. I quickly pushed his hands away and took him in my mouth, our eyes locked. Grabbing his ass with both hands, I sucked him as deep as I could muster. Ben cradled my head in his hands, rocking his hips forward, trying to get me to go faster, but I kept up my slow pace. He groaned each time he pulled back, my tongue dragging along the underside of his dick, just like I knew he loved. His eyes were closed against the sun, his mouth slack and the muscles of his torso tense. God, he looked beautiful.

"Oh god."

Those words usually signaled that Ben was close to coming and were my cue to stop. Taking the hint, I eased him back, his protests quickly quieted by my kisses. We stopped long enough for him to say the words I wanted to hear.

"I want you to fuck me, Cam."

He leaned his forehead against mine for a moment and I caressed him everywhere I could reach. Without a word, he turned away from me, his knees digging into the sofa cushion, his ass high in the air. I spread his cheeks apart, pressing the pad of my thumb against his puckered hole. He groaned, the sound slightly muffled by the fabric of the couch. Taking my time, I ran my tongue around his asshole, again and again, until he was squirming and pushing back against me. I reached for Ben's cock, but found his hand already there, moving at a frantic pace. He was trembling and my need for him was starting to get the better of me. I pressed the tip of my tongue hard against his center and we both let out a moan.

"Cam..."

I got up from the couch with the intention of heading to the bathroom when Ben stopped me.

"Where are you going?"

"To get what we need."

Ben pointed to the coffee table and smiled.

"The lube is under the metro section."

He stood up and I wrapped him in my arms.

"So, you were that confident you could get me to stay, huh Ben?"

He swirled his hips and I could feel the hard press of his erection against my leg.

"Yup."

"Cocky little bastard."

"I was right, wasn't I?"

He had me there. I kissed him and shoved him back onto the couch. Ben was back on his knees in no time, while I searched through the detritus on the table to find the lube Ben had hidden. I knelt behind him and he looked at me over his shoulder. Our eyes locked as I slid my lubed fingers over his hole.

"Cam, how much longer are you going to make me wait?"

His eyes fluttered closed as I pushed a digit inside him, a sigh the only sound he made.

"You didn't seem to be in such a hurry when you were trying to make me miss my train."

I twisted my wrist as I pulled out, making Ben moan so sweetly. When he spoke, it was barely a whisper.

"Am I being punished, then?"

I plunged my finger back inside him, as slowly as I could muster.

"Does it feel like punishment?"

He grunted, his ass coming back to meet me.

"It feels fucking amazing."

I leaned down over him and whispered right into his ear.

"Just you wait, baby."

I sat back and he looked at me as I lubed up my cock, his face impatient. He wasn't the only one desperate to get started. I pressed the head against his puckered asshole and I could see the tension run through Ben's muscles. Suddenly, he relaxed and let out a deep sigh as I eased inside him, his tightness enveloping me. The sun made his pale skin glow and as I ran my hands up his supple back, Ben rutted back against me, no longer willing to be patient.

"Fuck me, Cam."

With my hands firmly on his hips, I pulled almost all the way out, enjoying the way he whimpered as I did it. Each thrust of my cock made Ben moan, his hand wrapped firmly around his dick, jerking himself as I pounded into him slow and deep. I pressed my chest against his back, letting my teeth sink into the soft flesh of his shoulder. Kissing everywhere my mouth could reach, but it just wasn't enough.

"I want you on your back, Ben. I want to see you."

We eased away from each other and I waited as Ben rolled over onto his back, his legs in the air without a word. Before I could slide my cock back into him, he pulled me close, kissing me hard. He reached between us and guided me, gasping against my lips as I entered him. There was no more teasing, no more going slow. I started fucking him with abandon, his arms tight around my back. He lifted his legs higher and wider, allowing me just a little bit deeper inside him. I cried out when he scratched down my back, his hands coming to rest on my ass. He urged me on, writhing underneath me, forcing me to go faster. I eased away from him, trying to get some composure back, but his words took it away in an instant.

"Fuck, Cam. I'm so close."

As much as I wanted to keep us both in that moment, to hold on to the amazing tension for as long as possible, I was too close to stop. Ben's fist worked furiously around his cock and I felt him squeeze around me as he came, spurting all over his stomach, his cries turning into labored breaths. Watching him come always pushed me over the edge and I came harder than I had in a while, Ben's thumbs stroking around my nipples all the way through it. I collapsed on top of him, his skin so hot against mine. When my faculties returned, I tried to get up, but Ben didn't let me get very far, his lips tracing down the line of my neck.

"See, wasn't that better than getting on a train?"

I lay next to him on the couch, his arm thrown over my chest.

"It was okay."

His elbow dug into my ribs and I pulled him into a kiss before I continued.

"I do still have to go, Ben."

"I know. I got you a ticket for the nine twenty-two train."

I sat up and looked at him, but he was too busy reaching for my unfinished mug of coffee. He took a big sip and smiled.

"Oh, you did? Why didn't you just tell me that from the beginning?"

"Guess I forgot to mention it."

"Of course you did."

"You're not mad are you, Cam?"

I kissed him on the forehead and rumpled his already messy hair.

"No. But you really are a cocky little bastard, Ben."

"As if you'd have it any other way."

THE LAST ROMANTIC LOVER

Logan Zachary

September 28, 2009

Logan, blow out your candle and make a wish," Jake, my partner, said as he poured me another glass of champagne.

The waiter had just set a huge piece of Black Forest cake in front of me with a single candle burning on it. He stepped back, knowing full well not to sing "Happy Birthday" to me.

The Black Forest restaurant wasn't very busy for a midweek supper and birthday celebration, and I was glad. I looked into Jake's eyes and asked, "Jake, will you marry me?"

"Logan, you know until it's legal..." Jake set the champagne bottle back on the table and picked up his bubbling flute.

I raised my glass. "I don't care what the government says. I want to marry you, and a stupid piece of paper doesn't make my feelings for you any different. I love you, and I want to marry you." Our champagne glasses clinked.

"You want to drive down to Iowa and...?" He extended his fork to steal a bite of cake.

I nodded for him to help himself to the cake. "You don't understand. I don't care about some license or any silly documents. I want a pastor to marry us. In my heart, that's all that matters, not a stupid document."

"But if the paper doesn't matter..."

"Never mind. If you don't want to marry me, that's fine."

"I didn't say that. I just don't see why it matters so much to you. You're always such a rebel, you don't seem like the one to follow any ancient heterosexual ritual."

"I just want you to commit to me, and I want to commit to you. Why is that so hard to understand?"

"It isn't, but legally..."

"I don't care what they say. If I want to marry you, that's all that matters to me."

Jake took a big bite of cake.

"Fine, I won't ask you again, but once it's legal, you'll have to ask."

"Okay."

"And I expect a ring worth two months' salary." I raised my champagne glass and saluted him again before I drained it.

May 14, 2013

The newspapers said: *Governor Dayton Signs Bill Allowing Same Sex Marriages, in St. Paul, Minnesota.*

"So, are you guys going to get married?" Reed Williams asked, as the bartender set down the round of beers.

I laughed. "I asked Jake years ago if he wanted to marry me, and he said no."

Jake rolled his eyes. "Whatever." He picked up his frosty mug and tipped it to me.

Mark Simon leaned forward. "I don't believe that." He sipped the foamy head off his mug before he drank.

"I asked him and he said no, so if he wants to get married, he's the one who's going to have to ask me. I bought us matching rings." I held up my right hand to show them the silver ring.

"Why is it on your right hand?" Reed asked.

"I always go against the norm, you should know that by now." I drank a cold refreshing sip of beer and sat back on my stool.

"Jake, what do you have to say about that?" Mark asked.

"I'm not the most romantic man in the world, and Logan wants that. He wants me to fall on my knee and propose to him with a ring. He wants all that romance novel crap from me and…"

"He can't do it," I said.

"Can't or won't?" Mark asked.

I said, "Won't," as Jake said, "Can't."

February 14, 2014

"Supper was great. I can't believe you planned ahead for Valentine's Day." I stepped out on Hennepin Avenue and inhaled the icy night air.

"Well, the night isn't over yet." Jake snapped his fingers, and a horse-drawn carriage pulled up to the curb.

"What?" I'm sure the surprise was evident on my face.

Jake stepped aside so I could get in first. A thick, soft blanket was pulled over our laps, and the driver flicked the reins to get the horse moving.

I looked around the night sky as the buildings and street-lights flashed around us. A gentle snow began to fall, and the snowflakes sparkled and danced in the colored lights.

There was a pop next to me, and Jake held up a fizzing bottle of champagne and flutes.

I took one and held it as he filled it, and then the other one, as he repeated the process.

The Valentine's dinner had been a lot of fun, and so delicious.

Jake set the bottle down and turned to me. "To romance."

"To romance." I clinked glasses and drank, carefully eyeing the contents of the flute.

No ring.

We stopped at a red light and Jake took my almost empty flute and turned his back to me. Was this it? Was this the time?

He filled the glass and returned it to me, ringless.

I smiled and looked away.

Jake took a big swig of champagne and set his glass down. He knelt on the carriage floor and pulled the blanket up over his head.

He's down on his knee, he's down on his knee, my mind giggled, but my body felt my zipper lower and his hand digging me out of my pants.

My dick slipped into his mouth. The cold champagne and bubbles tickled every nerve. My ring was forgotten.

He swallowed the champagne and started using his wonderful oral skills on me. His talented tongue worked its magic, and I was rising to the occasion.

Jake pulled my hairy balls from my pants and rolled the fleshy orbs with one hand as he sucked on me. His other hand opened my waistband and carefully guided the pants down as far as he could get them.

I was in downtown Minneapolis getting the best blow job of my life.

He slipped a finger under my balls and explored deeper.

Closer and closer his tickling touch neared my tender opening.

I tensed my butt, as his tip brushed over my pucker. I almost shot my load then. He knew my body better than I did. He knew the buttons to push, stroke, caress and lick.

The pleasure was rising. I closed my eyes, unable to take the stimulation and the knowledge of what was going on underneath the blanket. A limo passed. A man nodded as he stood at the corner waiting for the light to change.

Could he tell what was happening? Did the driver know? Did he care?

I pushed away the thought of being arrested and let the joy grow and grow. I guided Jake's head over my dick. My fingers combed through his hair and held his head tight. I rocked my hips to match his head motion. I wasn't going to last much longer.

I usually moan and groan in the throes of passion, but being in the middle of Hennepin Avenue, my body language and gasping had to let him know I didn't have long to go.

He quickened his pace and plunged his finger deeper into me.

My balls released, and I shot my load down his throat.

He swallowed as fast as I came, sucking on my overly sensitive dick and driving me crazy.

I wanted to scream, "Stop!" and pull out of his mouth, but his tongue and his hands held me captive. He ravaged my body as wave after wave exploded out of me. My body jerked from the overstimulation as another spasm shot out of me.

Jake licked along my shaft and sucked hard at the tip as he finished. He popped up from under the blanket and smiled. He picked up the champagne bottle and refilled his and my flutes. He downed his glass.

Before I could say anything, he popped another bottle open and refilled his glass. He leaned over and kissed me.

I could taste myself on his lips as we kissed. "We're not going to be able to drive home after all this champagne." My head started to spin and I wasn't sure if it was from the champagne or the blow job.

"Good thing neither one of us works tomorrow. One more loop," Jake said, as he drained his flute.

"I'm getting dizzy," I admitted.

"Pull up your pants before you pass out or drop the blanket and expose something you shouldn't."

A party bus passed by, and several people shouted out the window.

I pulled up my underwear over my semi-hard dick and adjusted myself before pulling up my pants. I snuggled closer to Jake and felt his body heat radiate into mine.

He brought his arm around me and held me close.

Our loop of downtown ended in front of the Radisson Hotel on Nicollet Mall.

"We parked by Washington Avenue, not over here."

Jake carried the champagne bottle and his flute. "Take your glass and follow me." He walked through the revolving doors. He crossed the lobby and headed to the elevator.

I followed with my empty champagne glass. "Where are you going?"

"You'll see." His eyes sparkled as he pressed the button for the twentieth floor.

He pulled a card key out of his pocket and waited for the doors to open. Once we arrived, he walked to the right and stopped at 2013. The card key opened the door and a beautiful view of the downtown filled the windows in the room.

Two thick white robes were neatly folded on the king-sized bed. A Jacuzzi sat in one corner with another bottle of champagne on ice.

"We'll be staying here tonight." Jake removed his coat and folded it over the chair. He kicked off his shoes and started to unbutton his shirt. "Well, what are you waiting for? Get naked and we can hit the hot tub." He turned on the water and came to stand in front of me.

I looked into his eyes. My mouth was agape in surprise.

"Do you need me to help you?" He bent forward and kissed me. It started off as a peck and turned into a deep passionate kiss, mouths open and tongues exploring.

"I can't believe..." I started, and then he kissed me again.

His hands opened my jacket and let it fall to the floor. He tugged on my shirt and pulled it out of my pants.

My erection was back with a vengeance.

I stepped out of my shoes and reached down to unbuckle his belt and unbutton his pants. I didn't care that the curtains were open. Let Minneapolis watch. Soon, we stood naked in each other's arms, kissing and caressing. My hands kneaded his muscular butt.

The water level rose in the hot tub and Jake turned on the jets before he dimmed the room lights. The lights from the downtown buildings filled the room with a warm glow. The snow continued to fall in dancing flakes.

It was my turn to open the champagne bottle. I shot the cork across the room and filled our glasses as I watched Jake's beautiful bare butt crawl over the lip of the Jacuzzi. I swallowed hard as I stepped into the hot water with a raging hard-on.

The water bubbled hot around us and warmed us to the bone. Jake moved next to me and wrapped his arm around my neck as we soaked in the tub drinking our champagne. We stretched our legs out, and I felt my dick and balls float in the swirling water.

We looked out the window and watched the snow swirl around and float through the night air. The steam rose from the

Jacuzzi and beaded on our champagne flutes.

Jake emptied his glass and set it on the table by the tub. He moved to the center and slipped between my legs. His hard-on led the way to mine. They rubbed alongside of each other in the water. His hands combed through the hair on my chest as he kissed me.

My arms wrapped around him and pulled him closer. The hair on our balls tickled as it swirled between us.

Jake reached under the water and my legs. He spread them wider as he glided his hard cock lower and between my cheeks. He probed me, exploring lower.

I scooted my butt over the edge of the bench and gave free access to my bottom.

Jake's finger trailed along the crease and found my tender bud. He circled the opening a few times before he sought entry. Inch by inch his finger entered me. The hot water relaxed me and made for easy access. He slid in and out a few times.

I arched my back, and he knew I was ready.

He rose on his knees and guided his dick to my opening.

I pulled him closer and felt him swim into me. His thick shaft filled me as he slowly glided in. I held his chest pressed against mine in the bubbling water. I nibbled on his neck as his hands pulled my cheeks farther apart.

He repositioned himself in the Jacuzzi and was able to sink deeper into me. He rocked back and forth. We fell into an easy rhythm and enjoyed the slow ride back and forth. His hand brushed along my arousal, teasing the engorged flesh.

I thrust my dick toward him, begging him to touch me, take me, do me.

Before I could say anything, he lifted me up from the bench and twisted around. He sat on the bench and pulled me down on his lap.

I settled my feet on the bench and knew I was ready. I rode his dick, faster and faster. I thrust down on him harder and harder. I grabbed on to his pecs and found his erect nipples. I pinched the sharp points and twisted gently.

Jake moaned and found my cock in the bubbling water. He started to jack it as fast as I rode him. Harder and harder he stroked, as he plunged into me.

I threw my head back and let him have me, let him do anything he wanted. Pleasure rose along with the heat and the bubbles. The view of the city outside was blurred from all the condensation on the glass, but I didn't care; I was in heaven.

I felt Jake thrust into me one more time and a hot gush filled me. My cock exploded in orgasm as he squeezed it. I rose and fell on his dick again and another wave gushed out of me, and I felt his dick swell and spasm inside me.

The scent of male musk and sex filled the room and made me even more dizzy than the champagne. I rose and fell one more time and shot a last load before grabbing on to his body and hanging on for dear life, afraid I'd sink under the water and drown due to the drained feeling of my body.

We soaked in the steam for a while and the Jacuzzi turned off. Silence descended on the room, and we floated. Jake slowly pulled out of me and stepped out of the tub. He grabbed a robe and wrapped it around himself. He picked up the other one and held it open for me.

I stepped out of the tub, into the robe and into his arms. We walked out onto the balcony to cool off in the snowy night. Our breaths came out as a mist.

I turned to Jake. "And we haven't even tried the bed yet," I smiled, "or the shower, or the..."

Jake kissed me to stop my list.

July 20, 2014: Ireland

"Did you want the Black Watch pattern or the Stuart kilt?" Jake asked.

"What do we want these for?" I felt the thick fabric and marveled at the simple artistic design for such a fine kilt.

"We could use them as our Halloween costumes for Mark's annual party at the funeral home."

"Anything else?" I pressed. I remembered we had talked about getting married in kilts if the occasion ever presented itself.

"I've always wanted a kilt, and I'm going to get one. Did you want one to match or clash?" Jake knew me too well. "Let's go try them on." He headed off to the dressing room.

I followed behind watching his tight jeans hug his butt and wondering what his ass would look like in a kilt.

I stepped into the dressing room and kicked off my shoes and pants. It took me a few minutes to figure out how to secure the kilt. I wanted to be naughty, so I slipped off my underwear and stood looking at myself in the mirror. My hairy legs looked great in the kilt. Maybe I could pull this off.

The curtain pulled aside and Jake stood there. He looked like he had stepped off a romance novel cover. He just needed longer flowing hair and to take off his shirt, and he'd be perfect. Correction. He was perfect.

"Does my dick look big in this kilt?" I asked.

"No, your dick is big. Period."

I looked down at myself and did my best *Price Is Right* motion. "Ta-Da. I'll take it."

Jake smiled and pushed me down on the chair. He lifted his kilt and pulled the front up on mine.

My dick sprang to full length as I saw him flash me.

He guided his hairy butt over me and rode up and down my

shaft. He pulled out a small bottle and lubed up my dick before he lubed his backside. Our bodies rubbed against each other, hair crackling with static. Jake positioned himself over me.

I sat perfectly still as my tip found his tight opening. It was all I could do to keep from screaming as he slowly sank down on me. He sat still for a second, afraid I'd shoot. As that wave passed, he slowly rose.

My hand found his thick dick and stroked as he rode me. Deeper and deeper I plowed into him and my hand worked faster and faster.

He kissed me, and I knew this wasn't going to take long.

Jake doubled his speed, and I closed my eyes and clenched my teeth. He was so warm and tight and rubbed every nerve the right way.

My cock swelled, filling him even more, and then I felt my balls start to rise up.

"I'm gonna…" he panted.

I grabbed a tissue and caught his load as it shot out of his throbbing dick. I milked him, drawing out another wave of come. The hot, thick wetness triggered my balls to release. I plunged up and deeper into him and held my cock planted inside him. Eruption after eruption burst out of me and into him.

Another load came out of his dick and filled my palm.

He collapsed on me, his head resting against mine. He licked the drop of sweat from my neck, and he kissed me.

I gasped for breath and held him in place so he didn't move and stimulate any more of my overly sensitive nerves. I grabbed another tissue and handed it to him.

Carefully, he popped off me and sent another spasm out of my balls. He cleaned himself up before sneaking back to his dressing room.

I wiped up and quickly changed back into my own clothes.

My face burned as I exited the dressing room. My kilt was rolled into a ball.

Jake stepped out as handsome as ever with his kilt perfectly folded and held in front of him. He set it down on the counter and looked at the ball in my hand. Wordlessly, he took it and neatly folded it and set it on top of his. We went to the register, and he pulled out his wallet as the clerk rang him up.

I couldn't make eye contact, embarrassed that the clerk knew what we had done.

The clerk smirked and thanked us for shopping with him.

I jabbed Jake. "You're a bad boy. I can't believe we did that."

He kissed me and hooked my arm with his as we walked to the next store.

We entered a small shop next door to the kilt store, and I noticed the gold jewelry in the glass case as soon as we stepped inside. My eyes were immediately drawn to a beautiful gold ring with an intricate Celtic design. It was a thick gold band, perfect for a wedding ring.

Jake came and stood next to me. "Breathtaking, isn't it?"

The shopkeeper came over, opened the cabinet and took out the ring.

I slipped it on my finger. It fit perfectly.

"It was made for you," the man said in his thick Irish brogue.

"Maybe in another place and in another time," I said.

"Parallel time," Jake said.

"You've been watching too many of my *Dark Shadows* episodes."

Jake took my hand into his and rotated it to see all the sides. "You should get it."

"It's beautiful, but I already have a ring. I don't need

another." I took off the perfect ring. It seemed to vibrate in my hand as I gave it back. A cold empty feeling came over my body as we left the store.

September 28, 2014

We had a great meal at our favorite Chinese restaurant, hot sex at home, but no ring or marriage proposal.

Halloween Party, 2014

"Do we have to go this year? I really am not in the mood to go to the Halloween party." I complained the whole time I was getting ready.

"We have the perfect costume this year after our trip to Ireland." Jake stepped out of the shower. His golden body glistened with water droplets as he started to towel himself dry. He motioned for me to come over. He smelled of mandarin mango body wash as he kissed me to shut me up. His tongue slipped between his lips and into my mouth as I welcomed him. His hand reached down and patted my briefs-covered ass. "The kilts and tux coats will be perfect," he said as he broke our kiss, "but you have to lose these." He snapped the waistband on my Calvins. His hand slipped inside and squeezed.

"Commando?" I asked.

"Regimental," he corrected.

"Free-balling is still free-balling."

He slapped my butt. "Hurry up. We're going to be late." And he rushed off to get dressed.

The party was in full swing when we pulled up in front of the house.

"How did we get so lucky to have a parking spot right in front?" I asked.

"Must be our lucky night." Jake opened his door.

"Do we have to go? Can't we just go home and watch a movie?"

"We can't disappoint Mark. Besides, we don't have to stay long."

"Promise?"

"Promise." He crossed his heart.

I unbuckled my seat belt, opened my door and felt a cold breeze blow up my kilt. "That will wake you up," I said. I pushed the kilt down to maintain my modesty. "How do women get out of cars with skirts on without flashing all of their business?"

"Like a lady," Jake said.

"I don't do drag."

"Hurry up or you'll freeze your balls."

I bounced out of the car and adjusted my semi-hard on. I was partially aroused with this newfound freedom from underwear.

"Are you sporting wood?" Jake said.

"Maybe."

"Come on." Jake hooked my arm and we entered the party. We walked by the bar and grabbed a beer. Mark and Reed emerged from the crowd, dressed just like us.

"Hey, what's going on? Who are you guys trying to be for Halloween?" I asked. "Are you dressed up like us?"

Mark looked at Jake, who nodded at him. "Come with us and we'll explain."

"Where are we going?"

"The Chamber of Horrors," Jake said.

Something didn't ring true, but I went with it. The house was an old funeral home that Mark had remodeled into a huge residence. We walked to the chapel, which he had kept. All the beautiful stained glass and wooden pews and altar were too beautiful to remove.

The chapel was full and as the doors opened, all the zombies, witches, vampires and other monsters, stood and faced us.

Jake took my hand and looked into my eyes. "I know how much you love Halloween, and I know how much I love you." He dropped down onto one knee. "Logan, will you marry me?"

"We're your best man and maid of honor," Reed said, "but you can figure out who's who."

I couldn't speak, I couldn't breathe. I couldn't believe what Jake had pulled off.

"Is this romantic enough for you?" He pulled out a Barnabas Collins ring, silver, with a big black onyx stone, just like the one he wore in *Dark Shadows*. He slipped it on my right index finger. "It's not the real one, this is..." Jake pulled out the ring. The perfect, beautiful gold ring I had seen in Ireland with the delicate Celtic design engraved in the band.

"You didn't."

Jake simply nodded.

I looked at the altar, and our pastor stood up there waiting. This was all real.

So I did all I could do. I kissed him and said, "Yes," before I walked down the aisle with the last romantic lover.

INK STAINED

Krista Merle

The words aren't cooperating. Three days of effort and a blank page is lying in front of me, mocking me with its crisp, unbroken whiteness.

Never has starting a novel been so difficult. I pick up the top sheet from a small stack of papers lying next to me and read the few lines I've managed to pull out of my brain. Trite and melodramatic. I crumple up the paper, useless anyway, and stare at the ornate, carved bookshelf across the room. A tidy row of books with their leather covers and engraved front plates that all flowed effortlessly from my creative soul take up nearly an entire shelf.

This won't be the next one.

I want to throw a fit. In my younger days, I would have. The top of the desk would have been cleared off with a violent shove, the ink pot thrown across the room to shatter against the far wall leaving a spray of black like a bloodstain, and each of these ridiculous, infantile pages would have gone into the fire.

How my staff had hated me then.

And they were right to. I wish I could attribute my personal growth to age and maturity, but I can't. I wish I could say I've mellowed and realized that being rational is morally higher. But I can't. I'm a better man now than I was a year ago because of one person. A man who, despite being in my employ, has never once backed down from me or submitted to my demands.

Except when he's bent over my desk.

I groan at just the thought and my cock twitches. I wonder if he's in the manor somewhere. He should be, since I didn't send him on any errands this morning. I stand up, though a little awkwardly until I can rearrange the fall of my trousers.

Without even a cursory knock, the brass handle turns and the heavy oak door to my study opens, which can mean only one person. The man I was on my way to find.

"Oh good, you're not working," David, my majordomo, says as he walks in, his eyes riveted to the leather-bound appointment book that is never farther than arm's reach away.

"I was. It's not going as smoothly as I might have wished," I say, my eyes taking in every lean, wiry inch of him. His light hair is smoothed back and tucked behind his ears, and he's dressed in the same thing he wears every day, even though I never assigned him a uniform: black jacket and breeches with a soft white shirt and a simply knotted cravat. As he walks I can see leather patches on the insides of his knees, which makes me smile since I'd wager my fortune he's never been astride a horse. Tall black boots, polished so highly that they reflect the flickering light coming from the fireplace, encase his calves to just below his knee.

He makes a sympathetic noise and turns a page in his book. He still hasn't met my eyes, let alone nodded or, heaven forbid, bowed. He's lucky I don't stand on ceremony.

"God's sake, man, what is in that book that could possibly be so interesting?"

Finally, his eyes lift. Bright blue and deceptively innocent. I widen my stance, my shaft swelling already.

"I was just reviewing the market schedule for the tenant farmers and I'm concerned—"

Laughter from outside the door cuts him off and we turn to look. I lift an eyebrow at David and he sighs.

"The rest of the staff had a bit of a celebration at tea this afternoon," he says.

"Was there a reason for this celebration? Which, from the sounds of things, involved more than one bottle of my imported French wine? Men died bringing that across the channel, you know."

The corners of David's mouth curl up in a loose smile. He didn't look at all ashamed. "Perhaps just a few bottles. I joined your household a year ago. Apparently that's all the excuse they need to drink in the afternoon."

I laugh, feeling instantly more relaxed. Bugger the novel. This is far more important. "I suppose it has been a year already. I'm ashamed to say I hadn't thought of it." Which isn't the entire truth; I was very aware of how long he had been with me.

A year ago he'd presented himself at my front door and all but demanded a job. I'd been amused and, to be honest, a little taken aback. But more than anything I was intrigued. He'd proven himself smart and well-spoken but in the same way a pair of new boots shines—bright and clear, but without that broken-in patina. He'd been newly polished. I'd immediately wanted to scuff him up a bit.

In my mind, our real anniversary isn't for another three weeks.

He shrugs. "I hadn't thought of it either until I went down to the kitchen to talk to Cook about the next week's menu."

I walk around my desk and lean back against it, crossing my ankles. David's eyes sweep me, much like I'd admired him earlier, and his gaze catches at my crotch. I know he can see the strain on the fabric. I nod to the chair in front of me and David swiftly moves to it and sits down. He leans down and tucks the leather journal under the chair and, when he looks back up at me, his eyes are dark and intense.

"Seems like a milestone worth celebrating," I say.

David's reply is more of a hum than a word. It brings a swift shiver across my body. I know he hadn't come to my office for this reason, and that he could be so easily distracted, so easily seduced, does exciting and illicit things to me. He makes me feel strong and wanted. I may be a member of the peerage, but I never feel more powerful than when David lusts for me.

His hand lifts, his fingers reaching toward me but, after a year, I know him. I know he loves the game. So while I could simply open my trousers, pull out my cock and be buried in the warm wetness of his mouth, instead I step away. Just out of his reach.

I lower my chin and give him a chiding look. His full, bowed lips turn down and his eyes narrow. With a chuckle, I cross the room to the door. There is no danger of someone interrupting, the staff knows better, but I love the sound of the lock sliding into place. A dull thud that echoes through the room so pleasingly. It feels like I'm keeping him here, regardless of the fact that he wouldn't leave voluntarily. The sound signals a decision made, an action taken.

"John," he says from behind me in that voice he uses only when we're alone. So few people in this world use my given name. I love the way it sounds from him.

I wait, still facing the door.

I listen as his soft, padded footsteps bring him closer until I imagine I can feel the heat of his body against my back. His hands flutter against my sides and my eyes close.

"John," he says again, becoming more confident and sliding his hands up my back and to my shoulders. I'm taller, his head coming just to my collarbone, and he has to reach.

I turn in his arms and pull him against me, my cock pressed into his flat, strong stomach and his, just as hard, jutting into my hip. I groan and take his mouth in a hard, demanding kiss. My tongue presses between his lips and opens him so that I can sweep in, claiming my right to be there. His tongue is hot and rough as it tangles with mine. Our mouths press together, our breath mingling, as I walk him backward until his thighs bump into the carved edge of my desk. The desk rocks and the wax jack I'd used to seal a letter earlier falls out of its stand and rolls onto the floor.

I groan, suck his lower lip into my mouth and pull, scraping my teeth along the tender flesh. He shudders against me and his hands reach for the buttons of my trousers but I bat them away. I want him naked first.

Pulling my mouth from his, I take a second to drink in his lust-drunk expression. His eyes are hooded, his color high and his lips swollen from my kiss. He's perfect.

Without breaking our stare, I work the knot of his cravat free, one long, slow loop at a time. When it hangs loose, I pull one end so it slides from under the stiffened peaks of his shirt, revealing a slim triangle of skin that I can't keep myself from tasting. He tastes like he always does: clean skin, the tang of salt and a hint of the sandalwood soap I'd gotten him. An impulsive gift the first time when I'd seen it at the local market but I'd diligently kept him stocked with it since. Partly because I like the way it makes him smell but mostly because he likes it so much.

He stands still while I take my time undressing him, through the slow unbuttoning of his jacket and as I untie the laces of his shirt, though his hands keep curling into fists.

I brush the backs of my fingers across the front of his breeches, letting my fingertips hang on the knot in the drawstring, and David's breath catches in his throat. His eyes close and his teeth sink into his lower lip. I want so badly to kiss him but resist, dropping to one knee instead.

His eyes flash open and he looks at me, wide and surprised. I've only been in this position a handful of times before. It's not that I don't love his cock in my mouth, because I do, but I usually suck him from above. After making him beg for it. I feel a little unsure, but his eyes warm and his hand reaches out to brush my hair and I know the impulse was right.

Foregoing finesse and the slow seduction, I push his hips so he's leaning back against my desk and pull off his boots. My heart pounding, I unknot the tie of his breeches and run my palm along the outline of his thick shaft. The soft fabric is tailored close to his legs and I have to peel it down but, soon, he is finally, thankfully, naked.

I sigh and lean forward to kiss his hips where the bone juts against his skin. He shudders and holds on to my shoulders, his fingers digging in. He's wrinkling my jacket and I know I'll catch hell for it from my valet but I love it anyway.

"Please," he says, a soft, whispered plea.

Gripping his hips, I take his cock into my mouth and suck. Pulling back, I let him pop out of my mouth and admire the way the head reddens, then I suck him back in. I swallow him deeply, letting him hit the back of my throat every time I lean in. The round, smooth head glides across my tongue and his musky scent fills my head.

David's fingers tunnel into my hair and he moans loudly

as I work his cock. With one hand I reach between his legs and heft the weight of his stones. He groans and his hips shoot forward. When I feel him start to jump on my tongue and his balls tighten, I release him and stand up. I'm not ready for him to come yet.

Without a wasted movement, I unbutton my trousers and free my aching cock. A drop of wetness glistens at the tip and I watch David's eyes lock on to it. But that will have to wait. I need to be inside him.

"Turn around and bend over," I tell him and he complies immediately.

He pushes his ass up, two generous handfuls of hard muscle, and his feet are parted so I can see his heavy sac between his legs. I reach down and stroke my length.

I stretch over him, reach into the top drawer of my desk and pull out a little glass vial. It used to be an inkwell but when David came to work for me, I replaced the ink with olive oil from the kitchen. At first it was because he had me hard near constantly and I was bringing myself off every time he left the room. Then, one fateful day, I walked into my office and he was sitting in my warm brown leather chair, his jacket unbuttoned and his breeches pushed down around his thighs. His hand was wrapped around his cock and, as I watched, he stroked himself hard and fast, eliciting a throaty groan. I'd been frozen, lust overriding my every higher function. So lost in the moment, he didn't realize I was in the room until I was standing over him, falling on him like a hawk on a field mouse. After that, I started keeping this little vial around for times like these.

I pull out the stopper and tip it over him. A small stream of thick, dark yellow oil spills between his cheeks and makes his skin glisten. I catch some in my hand and smooth it over the length of my cock.

I step between his legs and slide my shaft between his cheeks, the oil warming between our skin.

"Yes, please, John," David says.

"Please what?"

He groans and buries his face in the crook of his elbow so his next words are muffled. "Please fuck me. Please give me your cock."

I throw my head back and swear. I needed that.

The head of my cock finds the puckered ring of his ass and I push. Harder. Until David gasps and pushes backward, impaling himself on me.

We both moan and I take a second to savor the feel of him, hot and so tight. Then I work my hips back and forth until I'm fully buried in him. Taking a firm hold on his sides, I rock back and forth, setting a fast pace. David vibrates every time I run against the bundle of nerves deep inside of him, like he's being rhythmically shocked.

Sweat pops on my brow and I fuck him harder, my eyes close and my breath comes fast, my world centered where we are joined.

"I'm going to come, John." David's voice is tight and desperate.

"No. Not yet." I stop moving, keeping myself seated deep within him until we both come down enough for me to pull out. "Turn over. I want you to watch."

David scrambles onto his back, his ass nearly hanging off my desk. Paperweights and pen nibs clatter to the floor and I chuckle. Here I thought I'd improved from my impulsive, younger days. The inkwell I'd been writing with had overturned at some point and David's arm is stained black from his elbow, along his forearm, all the way to his fingertips. I dip a finger into the pool on the desk and draw a line down David's chest, ending just above his shallow bellybutton.

Everything in my world is ink stained—my clothing, my furniture. Now he looks like he belongs to me.

I shed my jacket and pull my shirt off over my head, then take his mouth in another deep, wet kiss. Our chests meet, skin to skin, and heat flares between us. Lifting his legs so they hook over my hips, I reach between our legs and slide back into the warmth of his body. David groans into my mouth and I swallow the sound.

I try to keep our kiss going, my thrusts short and deep, but we are both panting within minutes.

I finally pull my mouth from his and say, "Look. Watch me fuck your ass."

We both look down and, silently, watch my rod slide in and out of him. His body accepting and grasping with each movement.

His cock jumps, leaving a smudge of wetness across his belly that smears the ink, leaving the head faintly stained. I reach down and grasp it, stroking him in time to my thrusts.

Greedy boy, he doesn't bother warning me this time, although I can tell he's close by the way his ass squeezes me. He comes hard, white jetting from him and covering both his stomach and my hand.

David lies back and pants, a murmured litany of prayers and curses falling from his lips.

I reach up and slide my coated fingers into his mouth. His eager tongue wraps around me and sucks, and it's more than I can handle. Shuddering, I orgasm deep inside of him. He sighs happily as his ass milks the last of my come from me.

I collapse onto his chest and feather kisses across his collarbone, down to his nipples and back up to the hollow of his throat. He grins and squirms as my breath tickles him and I scrape my teeth gently across his Adam's apple.

Leaning back, I'm about to pull out of his body when David crosses his ankles behind me, keeping me locked in. His fingers run along the curve of my ear and play with locks of my hair and I sigh.

I pick up my head and kiss him gently. My tongue dips into his mouth and I can taste the lingering salt of his spend. He looks so young and happy and simple, lying spread across my desk, his naked body still embracing my softened shaft. I lean over and pick up my pen, dip it into the spilled ink at David's elbow and write *for David* in large, flourished letters across a sheet of paper.

I have the dedication. The rest will follow.

BLUE HEART

Michael Bracken

I discovered a gray hair on Gary's chest this morning when I woke wrapped in his arms. As I stared at it I realized how much time had passed since I had first run my fingers through his chest hair.

We met as undergraduates at the University of Texas at Austin while George W. Bush was stumbling his way through his first year in the presidency. We weren't interested in Bush—in our bed or in our White House—much to the dismay of our fundamentalist parents, though mine ultimately proved more accepting of our relationship then Gary's. We were a pair of small-town boys who'd had to go along to get along through high school, even though we'd had no interest in feeling up the cheerleaders or banging the homecoming queen, and academics provided our escape from the confines of Southern Baptist narrow-mindedness. We'd reached the university from different Central Texas towns that were far more alike than their zip codes indicated, and didn't meet each other until fall of our senior year when we were a government major and an English major rolling burritos at a popular restaurant for the pocket change entry-level employment provided.

Gary, who wore his coal-black hair trimmed close to the scalp and who seemed unable to banish the permanent five o'clock shadow on his square jaw and strong chin, had played six-man football in high school. Three years later he retained the thick, muscular body of a football lineman. Though I often glanced at his firm ass and the bulging package accentuated by his tight-fitting jeans, I avoided displaying any obvious interest. My gaydar had proven woefully inadequate throughout my first three years at the university, and I'd had to talk my way out of too many embarrassing and potentially dangerous situations since moving to Austin.

I had been editor of my high school's newspaper, had been on the yearbook staff, and had avoided all extracurricular physical activities until my sophomore year of college when I discovered RecSports. I dropped my freshman fifteen through a combination of swimming and weight training, and continued use of the university's recreational facilities had toned and sculpted my body so that I was no longer the pudgy kid who'd graduated valedictorian. Even so, I retained a mental self-image of that pudgy kid, worried no one would be attracted to me, until those occasions when I caught a glimpse of my reflection and realized how much my body had changed during the intervening years.

My first three weeks on the job, Gary and I often worked the same shift behind the counter, rolling burritos for a never-ending stream of customers at the popular downtown restaurant that employed us. Our conversation, limited as it was, never became personal, so I had no reason to think he was interested in me until we were walking out of the restaurant at the end of our shift one Saturday night.

The restaurant had closed at midnight, and it had taken almost half an hour for employees to clean up, clock out and make our way out the back door. I had just reached my car and opened the door when Gary called to me.

"Dwayne?" He pronounced my name as a single syllable, not as two syllables the way my family and friends did back home.

I turned.

"Can I hitch a ride?" He explained that his car was in the shop after a fender bender with a clueless coed who'd been talking to her passenger when she plowed her car into the back of his at a stoplight near campus.

"Sure."

I climbed into the driver's seat and then reached across to unlock the passenger door. Gary climbed in beside me, provided directions, and less than ten minutes later I pulled my car into his apartment building's parking lot.

"You in a hurry?" he asked.

I shook my head.

"Want to come up for a beer?"

I had no other plans so I found an empty parking spot and pulled my car into it. Then I followed Gary into the building and upstairs to his second-floor apartment, a one-bedroom much nicer than the exterior of the building suggested it would be.

He led me into the kitchen, opened two bottles of Lone Star beer he retrieved from the fridge, and handed one to me. As I pressed the bottle to my lips and tilted it upward to take my first drink, Gary said, "I've seen you sneaking glances at my ass."

I quickly swallowed so that I wouldn't spit out my beer. I started to sputter a protest as I lowered the bottle from my lips.

He stopped me. "It's okay," he said. "I've noticed yours, too."

My cock twitched in my pants when I realized where Gary was headed with his comments. "You didn't invite me up here just to drink a couple of beers, did you?"

Gary put his Lone Star on the kitchen counter, stepped forward, and began unbuttoning my shirt from the top. By the time he pulled it free of my jeans and unfastened the final button, my cock had swollen with desire and pressed against the inside of my jockey shorts, yearning to be free. When Gary pushed my shirt off my shoulders, I set my bottle on the counter next to his and let my shirt slide down my arms to pool on the kitchen floor at my feet.

I wore no undershirt, and Gary must have liked what he saw. He took my hand and led me from the kitchen to the bedroom, where we undressed each other. The only light illuminating the room came from a streetlight half a block away but it was enough for me to appreciate the naked man standing before me.

Gary's perpetual five o'clock shadow should have been a clue, but I hadn't realized how hirsute he would be. Dark hair covered his chest, tapering to a treasure trail down his taut abdomen that led to a wild tangle of black pubic hair from which rose a cock thicker and longer than any I'd ever before encountered.

I couldn't believe my luck as I reached out and ran my fingers through his chest hair. Gary was everything I had ever imagined, and more. I'd dreamed about this moment, had toyed with myself in the shower while imagining various encounters with Gary, but had never expected to find myself in his bedroom. I had never been so aroused in my life, and my cock throbbed with desire and anticipation.

He reached for my erection and wrapped his fist around it. Before he could do anything else, I came, covering his hand with my sexual effluent.

We still laugh about it all these years later, but it wasn't so funny then. I was mortified. "I—I'm sorry," I stuttered. "I've never—this has never—"

"It's okay," Gary said as he released his hold on my rapidly deflating cock.

I'd fooled around with several guys, but had never progressed beyond mutual masturbation and blow jobs. They had been meaningless romps for no reason beyond simply getting each other off. Being with Gary was different. I had lusted after him for weeks, but more than that, he wanted more than a quick hand job.

He had a partially used tube of lube and a selection of lubricated condoms in his nightstand drawer. After he spun me around and had me bend over his bed, he slathered lube and my ejaculate into my asscrack. Then he opened one of the condoms and slipped it over his thick cock.

He stroked my sphincter until I relaxed enough that he could slip one lube-covered finger into me. After a few probing strokes, he removed his finger and replaced it with the head of his condom-covered cock, pressing firmly until I opened to him. He must have known he was fucking a virgin ass because he carefully eased into me until his entire length was buried in my shit chute.

I sighed with pleasure.

Gary grabbed my hips and drew back until only his cockhead remained inside me. Then he pushed forward again. He started slowly but moved faster and faster until he was pistoning into my ass with increasing speed and power. My flaccid cock slapped against my thigh with each of his powerful thrusts until I cupped my hand over it, and I felt my cum-covered cockhead paint my palm as it bounced in rhythm to Gary's pistoning.

My cock was just beginning to recover from my initial orgasm and was again swelling with desire when Gary came. He slammed into me one last time, moaning with pleasure as he held my hips tight against him and filled the condom with cum.

He didn't withdraw until his cock stopped spasming. When he did finally step back, he pinched the condom against the base of his cock so that it would not slip off as he withdrew. I turned, sat on the side of his bed and watched as he walked naked down the hall to the bathroom, admiring his tight ass and powerful legs. I heard water run for a moment and he soon returned with our beers but sans condom.

Still embarrassed from my premature ejaculation, I wasn't sure what to say. So I drank my beer, pulled on my clothes and told Gary I had to be going. He walked me to his apartment door without bothering to dress and he leaned against the open door when I stepped into the hall.

"See you at work?" he said.

"Yeah," I said. I couldn't look into his eyes, instead focusing on the thick cock that had been inside me only a short time earlier. I wondered if I would ever see it again. "Monday. My next shift is Monday."

As I drove away a few minutes later, I didn't know if our encounter was going to be a one-time hookup or if it would lead to something more. At home in the shower, my hand wrapped around my rejuvenated cock, I imagined future encounters.

During our shift Monday evening Gary made it clear that he wanted more, and the following weekend we had a proper date. His car had just come from the shop, so he picked me up and we went to a bar he knew on Sixth Street where we could dance and drink without being harassed.

Gary danced with me, held my hand and kissed me without hesitation, treating me as his lover and not his hookup for the evening. He introduced me to several other men at the bar, making it clear that he was a regular as well as that I was taken.

I'd never had any of my previous sexual playmates treat me as anything more than a fuckbuddy or worse, as someone for late-night assignations but not someone to associate with in the cold light of day. Gary made me feel special in a way no one else ever had.

Late that evening Gary took me back to his place, I didn't embarrass myself a second time, and I fell asleep in his arms after an abundance of mutual satisfaction.

That was only the beginning of our whirlwind relationship. By the end of the semester I was spending more nights in Gary's apartment than in my own, and our relationship, though it had started with a sexual encounter, developed into much more. After graduation we remained in Austin, choosing to cohabitate in the blue heart of a red state. Gary took an entry-level job working for the state of Texas while I found a position as assistant to the advertising director of a performing arts organization. During subsequent years I was promoted to advertising director and Gary had a meteoric rise through a series of government positions with increasing responsibility and commensurate pay.

Much like every couple that remains together for more than a dozen years, Gary and I went through several ups and down in our relationship—from financial struggles created primarily by crippling student loans to dealing with his family's complete rejection of him after we purchased a downtown loft together and they realized he wasn't just going through a phase. My parents grudgingly accepted Gary but made it clear they did not approve of our relationship. We found ways to survive the downs, making the ups even better, and along the way we found our place in the community.

We were social creatures, made friends easily and turned our loft into a gathering place for the capital's up-and-comers. Our dinner parties brought artistic aesthetes and government wonks together in ways neither of us could ever have imagined growing up in small Texas towns, and everyone in the know desired invitations to our holiday cocktail parties.

Despite multiple opportunities to stray—he with interns looking to curry favors and me with touring performers seeking little more than one-night stands—we remained true to each other, one of the core values we had learned from our families. Sometimes we told each other about the advances others made—from the most awkward to the most subtle—and used them to spice up our bedroom play, and sometimes we kept them to ourselves to fuel our own fantasies.

We still couldn't marry in Texas, but our relationship was as committed as any marriage in every way but legal. We had done all we could to let the world know we were a committed couple. What was mine was Gary's and what was Gary's was mine, with joint checking and saving accounts, joint ownership of the loft and both cars, and each other named as beneficiaries on our life insurance policies. Some of the things we did to cement our relationship were things we learned from our parents while other things we learned by watching the mistakes of our friends, many of whom ran through relationships like water through cheesecloth.

We settled into our early thirties confident in our careers and our social status but no longer the hot-bodied young men we had been when we met. The years had softened us both, but we still saw each other through a lover's eyes—a gaze that tightens flab and softens wrinkles, especially when we fail to wear our glasses or put in our contact lenses. Even so, I couldn't avoid the reality of the single strand of gray hair only inches from my nose.

As my lover snored lightly, I wondered what else might have gone gray. I pushed back the sheet covering us both and repositioned myself so that I could examine the neatly trimmed black pubic hair nestling his cock and ball sac. I soon found another gray hair spiraling outward from his left testicle.

Without my glasses, I had to get quite close to his crotch to see it and my warm breath must have tickled Gary's fancy. His flaccid cock twitched and began to rise, just as long and thick and magnificent as it had ever been.

I couldn't help myself. I wrapped my fist around the base of Gary's erect cock and took his swollen purple cockhead between my lips. I pistoned my fist up and down his stiff shaft as I traced the circumference of his glans with the tip of my tongue. Before long my lover moaned softly and shifted position ever so slightly.

I knew Gary was waking when I felt one hand on the back of my head and the other on my shoulder. I released my grip on his cock shaft and slowly drew the entire length of his cock into my mouth, something I had not been able to do when we first met. Then I drew back, stopping only when my teeth caught on the ridge of his swollen glans.

As I lowered my face to his crotch, I cupped his ball sac in the palm of my hand, covering the telltale gray hair. I massaged his testicles as my face continued bobbing up and down the entire length of his cock shaft and I tasted the first drops of precome.

My saliva and his precome dampened his pubic hair and slid around his ball sac to his asscrack. As I massaged his scrotum in my palm, I teased his sphincter with the tip of my index finger.

Soon Gary began bucking his hips up and down, thrusting upward to meet my descending face, and I knew he would soon come. When I suspected he was close, I pressed my finger hard against his saliva-slickened sphincter, pushing my finger in his ass up to the second knuckle as he cried out and came in my mouth.

I swallowed and swallowed again, and I held his cock in my mouth until it finally quit spasming and began to contract to its flaccid state. After I released my oral grip on my lover, I returned to the position I'd been in before I'd spotted his gray chest hair: his arms.

Gary stroked my hair and asked what had prompted me to rouse him from sleep the way I had.

I told him about the gray hair, how it had made me think of how young we'd been when we'd met, and how those thoughts had reminded me of everything we had shared during our time together.

"It's not the first gray hair," Gary said when I finished. "I've been pulling them out for weeks, hoping you'd never notice. If I had known this would be the result, I might never have pulled them out."

"Don't pull out any more," I told him as I looked into his eyes, seeing both the young man I had fallen for so many years before and the man who still made my heart beat fast. "Let me love you as you are."

UNWANTED FREEDOM

P. L. Ripley

C hance Marlow spent his last day of unwanted freedom in
O'Henry's Pub drinking enough boilermakers to kill the
desire to skip town. Tomorrow Tommy Bradley was being
released from a five-year stint in Hardaway Prison. Chance had
sent him there.

Running would be a smarter move than staying, but he had
to face Tommy like a man. They had, after all, been lovers for
more than a decade.

The door opened, filling the pub with an explosion of afternoon sunlight. Chance and the handful of other customers
squinted against the invasion. "Christ!" one of the old men at
the bar screamed, the shot glass in his hand quivering as he
brought it to his liver-spotted lips. The light reflecting in the
glass shimmered with a dull gray color. The old man was
drinking whiskey. It should have been a soothing amber. Chance
suspected the old man had been served mop water but was too
drunk to notice, or care.

The draw of O'Henry's was its lack of light. In the dark, Chance could forget he had once been happy.

Chance glared at the door as it swung shut, sealing off the light and the outside world. A silhouette filled the archway. It was a familiar shape. Tall, lean, with one leg cocked oddly to the side. The silhouette took a step and Chance realized it was Bennie, his oldest and closest friend.

Bennie limped into the pub, nodded his head at the men at the bar. They gave him a big hello and clapped him on the back as he passed them. Everyone loved Bennie. Maybe it was because he handed out blow jobs like they were sandwich coupons, or perhaps it was that he genuinely liked people and treated them with respect. Even when they didn't deserve it. Like Chance. He didn't deserve Bennie's friendship but was grateful he had it.

"Jesus Chance, you look like shit," Bennie said, pulling out the chair across the table. He dropped into it, keeping his bad leg stuck out from under the table, and massaged his knee. Bennie had his kneecap shot off in Afghanistan. A little reward for serving the current Washington administration, who, in all fairness, had inherited the war from the previous one. Though the current one was in no hurry to end that mess over there. Bennie was lucky it was only his kneecap that got blown away.

"Thanks man," Chance said and emptied his glass for the... what was it, sixth time now? Seventh? He didn't know or care. He just wanted to get drunk and it was starting to piss him off that he couldn't seem to.

"So, Tommy's coming home, huh?" Bennie asked and pulled his pant leg up to really get in good on that knee. His fingers worked the flesh. The plastic kneecap rolled and slid over the bone. Chance glanced down at the thin, hairy leg with the dragon tattoo curled over the shin, its mouth open, fangs dripping saliva or venom, looking like it was ready to take a bite out of Bennie's bad knee. He stared at that leg and wanted to feel it against his face. He wanted to run his tongue through that long leg hair, watch it clump with his saliva as he pulled those legs onto his shoulders and buried himself inside Bennie. He wanted to hear Bennie cry out his name as he pounded him to the fragile ledge of an orgasm, then push him over it. He wanted to feel the insides clamp down on him as Bennie came.

But, it would never happen. He knew that just like he knew he was in love with Bennie, and always had been. Bennie knew it too, that's why he would never sleep with Chance. "Good friends are hard to come by," he had said once when Chance proposed a bedroom maneuver. "If it doesn't work out, and it won't because I'm a whore, then we will end up with nothing. We won't be lovers and will no longer be friends. I don't want to lose you." Chance had thought it was a cop-out. That Bennie didn't want to risk feeling...something, anything. That's why Bennie had never been with anyone for more than a few weeks. He also realized Bennie was right. If it didn't work out then it probably would end their friendship. Reluctantly, he retracted his offer, but he still wanted him just the same.

"I don't know if he's coming home," Chance said, answering Bennie's question. "He is getting paroled. I'm just not sure where he's going to end up."

"Has he written to you?"

"No."

"In five years, he never wrote one letter? Not even a phone call?"

"No. I received a letter from the prison board that his parole has been granted, because I am his last address contact and..." he paused, struggling to verbalize the rest.

"The arresting officer," Bennie finished for him.

"Yeah."

"So, you're just going to what…sit here and get drunk and let whatever happens tomorrow when he gets out, just happen?"

"What am I supposed to do? Wait outside the prison for him?"

"Yes. That is exactly what you should do. Confront him. Find out if he does want to come home with you." Bennie stared at Chance. Their eyes bored into one another. "You do want him to come home, don't you?"

He did. That was the big kick in the teeth about the whole mess. He did want him to come home. He loved Tommy as much as he loved Bennie, if not more. He wanted him to come home so they could pick up their lives where they had left off five years ago. But he knew that was unlikely. He had arrested Tommy. He was the one who had held Tommy's hands behind his back and put on the cuffs. He was the one who read Tommy his Miranda rights, then dragged him from their home and shoved him in the back of the cruiser. How could Tommy ever want to come home to him after that? But then, how could Chance want Tommy after what he had done?

"I'd rather just get drunk. Maybe you will be nice and take me home. Maybe you will be really nice and let me suck you off before I pass out," Chance said, and he could hear his own voice slurring. The whiskey was finally kicking in. It was affecting him down below, too. He reached down and pulled the alcohol induced semi-erection from the crease of his leg and up onto his thigh.

"I'll take you home," Bennie said. "But that's all I'll do. We can drive up to Hardaway in the morning. You can hear it from Tommy himself if he wants to come back to you."

"And if he doesn't? What if he wants to kill me? I'm sure it's crossed his mind a few times in the last five years. I know, if I had been in his position, I would want him dead."

"You're a big boy. I'm sure you can handle him."

"I'm not afraid of him killing me, I'm afraid he will want to. I don't want him to hate me. Isn't that fucked? After what he did. Breaking into that old woman's house, tying her up and... Jesus, why do I give a fuck what he thinks? Why do I care if he's pissed that my testimony sent him away?"

"Because, you're just as crazy as he is."

"Perhaps. Maybe that's why we fit so well together all those years. All this time not hearing from him has given me the illusion that we can still be together when he gets out, though. That maybe he has forgiven me. Tomorrow, I guess, I'll find out what he really feels."

"You are the one that needs to forgive him. He is the one, after all, that...did what he did."

"I have. I forgave him the night I arrested him. He didn't kill anyone anyway. It was Sam who pulled the trigger on the old lady."

"If you forgave him, maybe it will all work out then."

Chance doubted it, but what option did he have but to hope?

After another couple of rounds and a slow, painful vomit session in the men's room, they stood on the sidewalk while Bennie hailed a cab. Chance weaved left and right in the fading sun, his eyes squinted against the light like a bat on his first day out of the cave. Dusk was coming, the streetlights flickered to life along the avenue, but it was still brighter out there than in the pub.

Chance squinted against the dim light, suppressed the urge to run back inside the pub. It was safer in there. There was booze still to be drunk in there. More importantly though, there were no reminders that Tommy was getting out tomorrow in there.

When they arrived at Chance's home, Bennie staggered him

down the hall to the bedroom. The same room where Chance had slammed Tommy against the wall and applied the cuffs. The same room they had slept and fucked in for ten years. Some nights the only thing Chance could see when he closed his eyes was the look of shame in Tommy's eyes as Chance asked him if he understood his rights as they had been read to him. Other nights he saw the look of bliss on Tommy's face as Chance made him come again and again. Both memories hurt now.

Bennie dumped Chance in the bed, pulled his shoes off for him and started to leave. "Stay," Chance called to him. "Please."

"I'll be back in the morning to take you to Hardaway."

Chance woke when he was pulled from the bed and thrown to the floor. He opened his eyes to see the intruder drop to his knees, the left one planted firmly in the center of Chance's chest, and shove a thin slice of steel to his throat.

"Tommy, you're home early," Chance said, not surprised to see his old lover.

Tommy grunted a hard reply. "No thanks to you, asshole."

Chance stared up at him a moment, waiting for the knife to pierce his skin, to tear into his larynx or slice into the jugular vein. When it didn't happen Chance said, "You look good Tommy. You've been working out."

Tommy had always been muscular from a lifetime of working construction. He was bigger now than the last time Chance had seen him, the day of the sentencing, five years ago. His chest was thicker, arms so fat with new muscle growth Tommy seemed barely able to keep them at his sides. They kept wanting to balloon out from him as though his hands were filled with helium.

"I didn't have much else to do, besides trying not to get raped or killed," Tommy replied, pushing the blade a little harder against the thin flesh. A tiny bead of blood welled up under the knife. Chance could feel it trickle down into the hollow of his throat.

"I'm sorry you had to go to prison. I'm sorry I had to arrest you," Chance said, and ran his fingers through the thick hair on Tommy's forearm. He traced the tattoos all the way up to the shoulder. Tommy had most of them before he went away, but there were a few new ones. A skull on his hand, a line through Chance's name on his bicep. "If you're going to kill me, just do it."

"You always were impatient," Tommy said and rose to his feet. He stuck out his hand for Chance to take. Chance accepted it, lifted himself from the floor and stood beside Tommy. It felt good to touch him again. He missed him more than he had admitted to Bennie. He was still powerfully, terribly in love with Tommy.

Chance slept in the nude. It felt odd standing naked with Tommy fully dressed. He turned, pulled a pair of white briefs from the dresser and stepped into them. Tommy dropped the knife on the end table, it clattered next to the alarm clock, then he sat on the bed. He huffed out a long sigh.

Chance sat, far enough away so they were not touching, but close enough to feel the heat coming from him, to smell the sweat and road on him. "I thought you weren't getting out until this morning."

"I got out on the twenty-eighth, yesterday."

"Oh. I must have mixed up the dates. I thought today was the twenty-eighth."

"Still can't read a calendar," Tommy laughed. "You were always bad with dates. I had to remind you when Christmas was coming up, remember?"

"Yeah. I remember," Chance said, his eyes suddenly filling with tears. A decade of memories came back to him all at once.

Ten years of birthday celebrations, anniversaries and holiday parties. Memories of just the two of them together, doing something unremarkable; eating dinner, cleaning the house, paying the bills together. The first time they made love. The relationship they had worked so hard to maintain, gone the moment Tommy decided to break the law.

"Hey," Tommy said, gripping Chance's chin and lifting his face. He wiped the tears from his cheeks and kissed him delicately on the lips. "I'm so sorry I did that to you."

"You're sorry?" Chance asked. He was the one that was sorry. If he could have lived that night over again, he would still have arrested Tommy, but not in their house. That was what bothered him more than anything else about that night. He should have met him somewhere neutral, the racetrack or O'Henry's pub. Anywhere other than their home. He had been afraid it would taint the place for Tommy. That even if Tommy forgave Chance for the arrest, he would not be able to step foot in the home they had shared for ten years because it was the place of his downfall. He was here now though, so maybe it hadn't bothered him as much as it had Chance.

"I was so mad at you. The first two years at Hardaway I spent planning your death. I not only wanted you dead, I wanted you to suffer just as I was suffering. I was your lover and you turned on me like some fucking rat." His face grew red with the ancient rage that had become new all over again.

"I realized though, you were right. I had gotten involved with some pretty shitty people. All I could see was the money. I didn't think anyone would get hurt. The old lady was supposed to have a million in jewels and cash in that place. I didn't realize she was Sam's grandmother, his only living relative. If we hadn't been caught, he would have inherited the house, everything in it and probably a hefty insurance check for what we stole. He killed his own grandmother for money because he couldn't wait for her to die naturally. She was in her nineties. How much longer could she have lived?

"I was such a fool," he continued. "I'm so sorry for cornering you into arresting me. I figured you might be the detective on the case. Part of me hoped you would be, that you would...I don't know, cover up my involvement in the theft. Sitting there in Hardaway for all those years though, I realized that if you had let me go, I would have hated you even more. You are a good cop. An honest cop. I tried to corrupt you."

"I'm not a cop anymore. I quit the night I arrested you," Chance said and scooped Tommy's hand into his own. "If you forgave me, why didn't you let me visit you?"

"Once I realized you were right to do what you did, so much time had passed. I thought maybe you had moved on. Found someone else. Forgotten about me. I kind of hoped you had. I thought maybe Bennie had finally come to his senses and...and you were happy. That's all I hoped for in there. That you were happy, even if it wasn't with me."

"There is nothing between Bennie and me."

"Only because he won't let it. I know you love him, and you always have."

"Maybe." Chance said, averting his eyes from Tommy's for a moment.

Tommy moved in closer, pressed his lips to Chance's, then backed away. His nose wrinkled. "You stink. When's the last time you bathed?"

"I don't know. What month is this?" Chance asked, lifting his arm and giving his own pit a good sniff. He did stink. The funky odor of very old sweat wafted off him. He could also smell the booze he had wallowed in a few hours before rising off him like a morning fog.

"Were you in O'Henry's getting drunk tonight?"

"Yeah, a little bit," Chance replied.

"Are you still drunk?"

"Yeah, a little bit," Chance repeated.

"Come on. I'm getting you in the shower," Tommy said and pulled Chance to his feet and yanked the briefs Chance had just donned down to his ankles. Chance stepped out of them and let Tommy lead him to the bathroom. He waited patiently as Tommy turned on the water in the tub, ran his hand under the stream until it reached the right temperature, then flipped the lever to direct the water out the showerhead.

Chance stepped in the tub, let the hot spray pulverize his skin. It felt good, the quick, needle-like stabs of hot water cleansing him. Tommy pulled his own clothes off, dropped them on the bathroom floor, then joined Chance in the shower. He drew the plastic curtain closed and grabbed the bar of soap from the recess in the wall. He hugged Chance from behind while he ran the soap over Chance's chest. He massaged the soap into his skin, working the bar down over Chance's cock and letting it slide up into the crack of his ass.

Chance leaned into Tommy and let him wash him. He felt Tommy's hands scooping down between his buttocks, the finger sliding into him. The soap burned, but the penetration felt good. Tommy's hands grabbed at Chance, tugged on him, stroked him until he was standing to full attention. "Fuck me," Tommy moaned and turned, facing the wall. Chance turned, slid inside Tommy until his balls rested lightly against Tommy's own low-hanging testicles.

It was incredible, so warm in there, and tight. It was like coming home after a long day. The familiar way Tommy pressed back against him, wanting more and more of Chance inside him. The shivery little sigh as his cock rubbed against

Tommy's prostate, working faster, pounding him to a hard, whimpering cry as the orgasm built inside him. He knew just where to touch Tommy to bring him pleasure. Knew how to twist Tommy's nipples and yank on his hair as he slammed into his lover, harder and harder, until his own groin was battered and bruised. Tommy liked it rough and Chance was always eager to love him that way.

Chance looked down at his bare cock sliding in and out of Tommy and he wondered how safe this was. Did Tommy play safely in prison? Did he ever take a chance and have unprotected sex? He could not have been celibate for five years. Tommy always wanted it several times a week, often needing it daily. He couldn't go five years without it, could he?

Chance himself had not been celibate. He never brought a man here, though. He wouldn't infect their home with another man. He had kept his indiscretions to the back room of the leather bar or traded blow jobs through a glory hole at the adult book store. The release had eased his tension, yet the orgasms made him feel empty. He had often thought of Tommy when he came and it had made Chance miss him even more. He would lie in bed, staring up at the black ceiling, wishing he was in that prison cell with Tommy, then realizing he was in a cell of his own. His solitary life had become his prison. Now he had been paroled.

He trusted Tommy though. After all he had done, after breaking into that old woman's house and screaming at Chance in the courtroom that he wanted him dead, he still trusted him. Tommy wouldn't risk his own life just to come.

He pushed himself harder, deeper into Tommy, feeling the warm passage milk him. The channel churned and convulsed as he pounded Tommy's prostate, bringing him closer and closer to his nut-busting end. "Fuck me, Chance," Tommy groaned, his voice gurgling as the hot water sprayed over their backs, filled his mouth. He spat it out, ran his fingers over his eyes to clear the soap and water and stringy clumps of dark hair. He pressed his hands against the tub wall, pushed back. His ass gobbled more of Chance's cock. He always wanted more, no matter how much Chance gave him. He was a greedy fuck and he fucked greedily.

Chance grabbed Tommy's dark hair, pulled it until his neck snapped back, head tilted at the ceiling. He leaned in and bit Tommy on the ear, feeling the skin pop as his eyetooth punctured the lobe. He could taste blood. Tommy yelped and shoved himself backward, slamming Chance into the wall. The hot and cold water dials slammed into his back, the showerhead raked his own head. Pain shot though Chance's body like an explosion. Chance grunted and shoved Tommy hard. The two men tumbled and slipped on the slick tub floor and spilled out of the tub, bringing the plastic curtain with them.

Chance had slipped from Tommy's body. Tommy was on his back, the curtain spread out beneath him like the rubber sheet they had used for the water-sports games they had played on occasion. Chance climbed on top of him, pushed his legs up and shoved himself back inside Tommy again. He entered him without care or ceremony, just set the head against the wrinkled hole and shoved his way in. Tommy yelped, but didn't pull away. He liked it like this. Hard, rough, angry.

Chance held himself up with his arms locked at the elbows, hands on either side of Tommy's head. He stared into Tommy's eyes as he pounded away at him. There was light staring back at him. It was a warm glow, loving. It made Chance feel welcome, like the happy yaps of the puppy he had as a kid when he came home from school. This was home, the house surrounding them and the body engulfing him.

He loved him more now than he had ever before. Tommy had come back to him, even though Chance didn't think he would have returned if the roles were reversed. He didn't think he could swallow his pride and admit he was wrong, like Tommy had.

He was close now, so dangerously close to coming he turned his eyes from Tommy's and filled his head with unpleasant images. He saw Tommy screaming for his blood in that courtroom five years ago. He saw the anger and pain of betrayal in his lover's eyes directed at him. His erection began to wither. Chance shook the images from his mind, stared back down at those same eyes, filled with love and ecstasy for him now instead of hate. Everything came back to him harder and stronger.

He needed Tommy to come before he could. He lifted his hand from the floor, slid it between them and took Tommy's cock in his palm. He stroked it with the same rhythm he pumped Tommy's ass, like a well-choreographed dance. Water dripped from Chance's face, raining down on Tommy as they grunted, pushed and pulled at each other.

It only took a few stokes before Tommy let go. He lifted his hips, bucked against Chance as he came. The hot wet splash shot up over his chest, arcing in the air with the force of five years of want. Chance caught some on his tongue as it flew between them, like a kid catching snowflakes. He swallowed it and wanted more. A gob fell on Tommy's mouth, sealing his lips. Chance leaned in, lapped the come from his face as Tommy's insides clamped down on him. It was all over for Chance. No man could take the pressure he was feeling and not lose control. He came with the same violence Tommy had. His entire body spasmed and he saw nothing but a hot white cloud and Tommy's eyes floating in the mix. He collapsed on top of his lover as his balls continued to empty, filling Tommy to overflowing. He sat back, slowly pulled his cock out of the pulverized hole and watched as what seemed like gallons of his seed trickled out, pooled on the shower curtain.

Tommy sat up, dipped his finger between his legs and pulled a thick gob of Chance's come from the curtain. He popped the finger in his mouth. "I've missed that. You taste so good," Tommy said and pulled another finger full from the wet plastic. He held it before Chance. Chance opened his mouth and let Tommy feed him.

Tommy said, "Thank you for bringing me home again. I wasn't myself for so long. Doing what I did just showed how far from myself I had gotten. You brought me back."

Chance stood, turned the water off in the shower, then picked Tommy up from the floor. He was heavier than before, but Chance carried him into the bedroom just the same. He gently set him on the bed. This time, they were not so forceful, not as hungry for an orgasm. Chance explored Tommy, touched him everywhere both with his hands and his tongue. He sucked the water from Tommy's skin and traced the new tattoos with his fingers. He stared at his own name, the thick, black line running through it. Tommy glanced down at the altered tattoo, averted his eyes from Chance's. "I'll have it fixed," Tommy said.

"If you want," Chance said and slipped himself inside Tommy again. He wasn't rough. He didn't pull Tommy's hair or drill him like he was searching for oil, but slowly pushed back and forth inside him, letting the rush of his cockhead tickling Tommy's prostate do all the work.

Hours passed as the two men touched, kissed. Chance slowly rocked his hips, working his cock back and forth inside Tommy. "I love you," Tommy moaned.

Chance came, not with a hot flash explosion but a ripple like a pebble tossed in a lake. It seemed to go on forever. "I missed you," Chance said once he could speak again and they held each other as sleep took them.

Chance woke when he heard the front door open then close. He looked over at the other side of the bed, expecting to see Tommy had left. He was still there. His hair had dried to dark, standing spikes. The clock read 6:00 a.m. It had to be Bennie out there, ready to take him to Hardaway prison.

Chance slipped out of the bed, donned the pair of underwear Tommy had removed from him before ushering him into the shower and quietly crept out to the kitchen. Bennie was leaning against the counter. He had a Styrofoam cup of coffee in his hand. Another sat on the counter. "Good morning," Bennie said. "Hungover?"

"A little. Tommy came home last night. I got the dates wrong."

"Are you all right?"

"Yeah. We had a good night," Chance said. He felt the smile splitting his face. It felt good to smile again. To be happy again.

"That's great," Bennie replied and pulled Chance into his arms. Chance hugged him back, tightly. He could smell the fresh shampoo in Bennie's hair. He didn't want to let him go. He loved Bennie so much it often hurt. But he loved Tommy just as fiercely.

No, he realized just then, he didn't love Bennie the same way he loved Tommy. He had gone five years waiting for Tommy to get out of prison, barely even looking at another man the entire time. He had quickly forgiven Tommy for fucking their lives up, for the crime he had committed and the incarceration that followed. He had been alone all that time waiting for Tommy to come home, not even sure if he would return to him.

He was not sure if he would have done that for Bennie. He loved him, but it was not the same.

Bennie pulled himself out of Chance's arms. "Well, I guess we don't have to drive to Hardaway now, do we?"

"No. Thank you for getting me home last night."

"Anytime. Give Tommy my best. He's a lucky man, you know that?"

"Maybe I'm the lucky one," Chance said, knowing it was true.

Bennie left and Chance went back to the bedroom. He climbed in the bed, curled himself around Tommy, felt his steady breathing and regular heartbeat thumping in his chest. Tommy moaned, rolled over. His head rested on Chance's chest. Chance wrapped his arm around him, hugged him even closer. He buried his face in Tommy's hair, kissed the top of his head. Tommy was out of prison; Chance's unwanted freedom was gone.

Finally, after five years, they had both come home.

A RIDE HOME

Brent Archer

1992

Bryant Thalman stepped off the bus, pulse racing as his anxiety skyrocketed. He checked his watch. *Shit. Twenty minutes late. Damned buses. I'll never get the system down.* He took in his surroundings in the unfamiliar neighborhood. The low brick buildings all looked the same. One story, large windows, and all attached to the next. Searching each one for its number, he sighed in relief at the blue awning with large white letters on it a block away—DANCE ON CAPITOL HILL.

So that's what they meant by "The DOCH" when they sent the rehearsal invitation. He hurried across the street and down the block, opening the glass double doors and peering in as his eyes adjusted from the bright sunshine outside. To his right, a tiled hallway led to a small sandwich shop. Music floated up the stairs in front of him, so he descended to the lower level and found locker room doors next to two dance studios.

Change and bathroom break before dancing. He pulled open the door.

Bryant's jaw dropped at the sight that met him. A tall dark-haired man faced away from him with fingers hooked into rapidly descending jeans and underwear. A taut ass dusted with dark curly hair spread in front of him. His eyes grew wide as saucers and fiery heat rose in his cheeks.

The undressing dancer jumped, apparently realizing the door had opened. He spun to face Bryant with his eyes wide, face red and hands covering his cock. "Oh, sorry, I'm just changing into my jock."

Their eyes locked and Bryant's chest tightened. Warmth spread across his body. He'd never in his eighteen years experienced this feeling. The lean athletic dancer before him had full lips and eyes the color of his green T-shirt. A tuft of curly dark hair peeked over his collar, and a dark thatch of hair poked out from under his hands and led to long muscular legs.

He grinned. "Mind closing the door? There's a bit of a draft."

Bryant snapped out of his daze as his eyes again swept over the hunk in front of him. "Oh, sorry. You just took me by surprise." He pulled the door shut and then scurried over to an open stall. Slamming the door shut before the stud could see the erection rising in his jeans, the flustered teen stood with his back against the stall door. *Whoa, what a stud.* He took a couple of deep breaths to slow his racing heart and opened his dance bag, pulling out a pair of black shorts and a tan T-shirt.

The door to the locker room banged shut as Bryant changed his clothes. He cracked open the stall door and peeked into an empty room. Shrugging his shoulders as disappointment settled over him, he stepped out of the stall. *Probably in the other studio. I'm so late I can't imagine he's one of the dancers in my group.* He left the locker room and took a deep breath as he walked into the rehearsal.

The only familiar face was Tony from the audition a couple of months prior. Older, with long blond hair and piercing green eyes, he greeted him warmly. "Bryant, so glad you made it."

"Sorry, I'm trying to figure out the buses and missed the first one."

Tony's hand clasped Bryant's shoulder with a strength that made the young man wince. "No problem. Let's get started." Tony introduced him around. Bryant's smiled faded a bit when he didn't see the handsome stranger from the locker room amongst the dancers.

They partnered up, and the lines started moving. The tall sweet woman, Anne, took his hand and placed hers on his shoulder. "I'm glad to meet you. Looking forward to performing with you."

"Thanks. I think this'll be a fun diversion from my studies."

He concentrated on the moves until suddenly the sexy stud from earlier danced across the floor in front of him. Bryant's breath caught in his throat as he tripped over his feet. His partner grabbed his arm.

"Sorry, Anne, I lost my concentration for a second. I'm not usually so klutzy."

"No problem." She glanced over his shoulder and gave him a smirk. "There are a few distractions for your dancing as well as your studies in this studio."

Heat rose again in his cheeks as he spun her around the floor. *Concentrate on the dancing, not on your dick. Geez.*

Over the next hour, Bryant struggled to keep up with the rest of the group. The dance moves were unlike any he'd attempted before, and he dripped with sweat. The stolen glances at the hot stud from the locker room didn't help the heat flowing through his body. Between choreographies, the overheated teen gawked as the older hunk bent over to stretch his legs. Bryant dropped to the floor and reached his arms for his outstretched legs to hide the erection pushing against his shorts. He'd have to figure out how to make his cock behave during rehearsals.

At the break, the object of his desire approached Bryant. "Hi, I'm Alan." He put out his hand. Bryant grasped it and the sizzling touch sent a shot of lust through his arm and down to his crotch.

"Bryant," he croaked. He held Alan's hand, mesmerized by his green eyes.

Alan smiled. "I'm gonna need that back before we start up again."

Bryant relaxed his grip and Alan withdrew his hand. "Sorry. You weren't here when Tony introduced me to everyone."

"Yeah, I had to run back to the truck. I left my dance shoes out there."

On the other side of the studio, Tony clapped his hands together. "Okay, break's over. Let's run the last routine again."

The sexy stud turned back to him with a wink. "No rest for the wicked."

Bryant melted as Alan turned away to take a sip from his water bottle. Another view of that luscious ass sent the hot and bothered young man into overdrive as he willed away his erection.

They rehearsed for another two hours. Each glance at Alan sent shivers up his spine and jolts of erotic energy into his cock. Finally he closed his eyes and let out a deep sigh. *Stop looking at him, or you're gonna pop a boner and humiliate yourself.*

At the end of the afternoon, the exhausted teen flopped down onto the bench by the door, panting. *Four-hour dance rehearsals. What was I thinking joining this company?* He checked his watch as his stomach grumbled. *Great, another hour before the bus, and then forty-five minutes more until I get to eat crappy dorm food.*

Alan sat down next to him. "You looked great out there. Have you performed before?"

His heart raced again. "Yeah, I danced in high school, and now that I'm at university, I want to continue. That's why I auditioned for the group. I'm not sure I'm cut out for the long rehearsals, though."

"What? You did great out there. It just takes some getting used to. You'll be fine."

Bryant glanced at him, and then turned away. "That's nice of you to say, thanks."

They were quiet for a moment as Bryant played with his fingers, nerves preventing him from starting another conversation.

Alan turned to him. "Hey, I'm sorry about earlier. I usually use one of the stalls, but being late, I just dropped my pants. I'm sure you didn't want to see my hairy ass when you opened the door."

Heat rose into Bryant's cheeks. "It's fine."

Alan arched an eyebrow and grinned. "Oh really? Well, thank you."

Heat surged from Bryant's cheeks to his toes. Suddenly the room got a lot smaller, and he glanced at the door as he stood and spluttered his response. "Uh, I'd better get going to the bus stop."

"When's the next one?"

Bryant looked at his watch and sighed, sitting on the bench again. "Forty-five minutes."

Alan stood and extended his hand. "How about you come

to dinner with me and then I'll take you home. You're at the U, right?"

"Yup." Anywhere this handsome guy wanted to take him had to have better food than the dorm. Besides, a better opportunity to get to know Alan probably wouldn't present itself. "You don't mind that I'm a sweaty mess?"

"I don't mind if you don't. I'm a bit of a mess myself. I know a great pizza place that won't care."

"You sure?"

"Yes, it's on my way."

Decision made, Bryant smiled, flushing with warmth and pleasure. He took the offered hand and pulled himself to his feet. Sparks of desire flew between them as they made contact. "I'd like that a lot."

1997

"What the hell do you mean you promoted him?" Bryant's boss Llewellyn Fiske pushed his massive frame across the room, passing Bryant's desk with an angry glare. He strode into his office and slammed the door, the artwork on the wall shuddering as the crash sounded throughout the office.

Bryant hung his head. *Fuck, why did I put in for that promotion?*

Jeri, the executive assistant to all the lawyers on their floor, hurried to Bryant's desk. "I'm so sorry. Not exactly the way you wanted to celebrate. I think it's great you are moving up."

Bryant turned to her. "But Jeri, the idea was to be able to bill for my time. I don't get why he's so angry."

Jeri put her hand to her forehead. "You're not the first person to get promoted out from under him. It'll be fine, I promise."

Just then, Llewellyn opened his door and stuck his head out. "You." He pointed his stubby finger at Bryant. "Don't you *ever* bill *anything* for *any* of my clients." One more nasty glare, and he slammed his door shut again.

Jeri chewed a fingernail. "Oh dear."

Bryant burned. *Bastard. Now what the hell do I do?* He pushed his chair back and stood. "I'll see you later, Jeri. I need to clear my head." He walked down the hallway toward the firm's HR office. *First job out of college. Shitty pay, I'm bored to tears, and now the boss makes it impossible for me to do my job. Fuck him, and fuck this place.*

He reached the door. Tracy looked up from her desk and smiled brightly. "Hi, Bryant. Congratulations on your promotion. You really deserve it."

Bryant stood in the doorway leaning against the frame, still on fire from the boss's tirade. "Llewellyn doesn't think so. In fact, he's decided in rather a spectacular fashion to not allow me to bill for any work I do for his clients."

Tracy's face fell. "What?"

Bryant's blood boiled. "Yup, that's what he said as he pointed his finger at me and yelled."

"Shit."

Bryant stood up straight. "I really appreciate you going to bat for me, but I can't stay in this kind of environment. I told myself I'd never work for someone who screamed at me. He's crossed the line, and so I'm putting in my notice."

"Bryant, please don't do that."

He crossed his arms. "Two weeks from today will be my last day."

"Is there nothing I can say to change your mind?"

"No."

Tracy nodded. "I understand. I'm so sorry."

"Me, too."

* * *

Bryant got off the bus and walked the block to his apartment. Still angry, he fumbled with the key to the outer door and dropped it on the ground. *Fuck.*

"Hey handsome, what's new?"

Bryant snapped his head up. Alan walked toward him with a smile and a bouquet of bright yellow daffodils. Bryant's shoulders dropped and some of the weight he carried slid away. "I'm so glad to see you." He set his backpack onto the sidewalk, and wrapped his arms around Alan's torso.

"Hey, baby, what's wrong?"

Bryant nuzzled his face against the fabric of Alan's dark-blue sweater. He inhaled the scent of ground coffee beans, and squeezed him tighter. "I got my promotion."

"Hey, that's great. Let's go celebrate."

"I quit my job."

Alan pushed him back far enough to look into his eyes. "What?"

Bryant sighed. "The boss went berserk when he found out. I guess they didn't consult with him before making the decision. He basically cut me off at the knees and made the promotion worthless. What use is a document clerk that can't bill for his time?"

Alan shook his head. "Fucking lawyers. I'd never work for a law firm."

"He thought yelling at me was a good idea."

Alan pulled him back against his chest. "Well, it is definitely their loss. You don't want to work in a place like that. I still want to take you to dinner."

Bryant rested his head against Alan's chin. "What am I going to do? I just got a notice that rent is going up a hundred and eighty a month. I couldn't afford that *before* I quit."

Alan kissed the top of his head. "Let's take this inside. You can put your stuff away and we can talk about it."

Bryant reluctantly pulled away and retrieved his key from the ground.

"Mmm, I love it when you bend over."

In spite of his worry and stress, he laughed, putting his hands on his knees in mid bend to steady himself. Turning to Alan, he grinned. "You always know the right thing to say."

He unlocked the lobby door and checked his mailbox. Alan took his hand and squeezed it. Bryant glanced at him and smiled as they walked down the creaking hallway. Bryant looked at the faded paint on the wall as he inhaled the musty scent of the carpet. *Maybe it's not a bad thing to find another place. This building hasn't improved with the new owners.*

They reached his apartment, and Bryant unlocked the door. Alan held it open for him, and they went inside. He dropped his backpack onto the table and sat down on the futon couch against the wall.

Alan pulled a chair from the dining room table and placed it opposite him. "This isn't the end of the world. In fact, it's a fortuitous change of events."

Bryant's shoulders tightened as his brow furrowed. "What do you mean? I might have to move back in with my grandparents in Spokane. If I leave Seattle, I likely won't be able to come back."

Alan's eyes widened. "That can't happen."

Alan's words took a moment to register through Bryant's haze of worry. He raised an eyebrow. "Why's that?"

"Because I love you."

Bryant's mouth dropped open. "What?"

Alan smiled. "I love you, and I want us to be together. So here's my proposition. Move in with me. My apartment has two bedrooms. You can put your stuff in one of them, and we can have hot monkey sex in the other as often as we want."

Speechless, Bryant put his hand to his forehead.

Alan leaned forward in his chair toward the shocked young man. "We can do two months before you need to worry about helping financially. That'll give you plenty of time to get a new job. You're smart and resourceful, so I've no doubt you'll land something quickly. My sister moved out three weeks ago, so there's plenty of room."

Bryant's face flushed with warmth. Alan wanted him. Truly wanted him. He thought about their friendship, and how much he enjoyed their time together. He knew he loved Alan, no question in his mind.

"Are you sure? I'm starting over from nothing here."

"No you're not. You have a college degree, work experience and all the sex you could possibly want. You only need a good man to come home to every night. That's what I'm missing, too. We already spend a lot of time together. Let's make it official."

Bryant fought down tears as he pushed forward off the futon and kneeling on the floor wrapped his arms around Alan still seated in the chair. "Thank you."

Alan kissed him hard and gently bit his earlobe. "How about we pull out the futon and consummate the deal?"

A shiver of lust traveled down Bryant's spine. "Yes," he hissed as his lover nibbled at his neck.

Alan pulled away and they stood. He cupped Bryant's face in his hand, sparkling green eyes dancing with desire. "I can't wait to sleep with you wrapped around me every night."

A tear slid down Bryant's cheek. "I love you."

Alan's smile lit up the room. He wiped away the tear with his thumb and pulled Bryant into another embrace, squeezing him tight. "I love you, too."

2013

Bryant took off his suit jacket and hung it on a hanger in the expansive closet of the hotel room. The ring on his finger glittered in the light, and he stopped to admire it. Ten diamonds inset into a gold band.

Alan strode out of the bathroom with a towel wrapped around his waist. "Hey there, what are you thinking about?"

Bryant raised his eyes, savoring the view of the man he'd stayed head over heels in love with for all these years, and grinned. "Just thinking how full of shit you were."

Alan raised his eyebrow. "Oh?"

Bryant chuckled. "Yeah. When you told me that taking me home was on your way. What a lie! The U is a mile and a half in the opposite direction."

Alan took the towel from his hips and ran it over his salt-and-pepper hair. "Well, I didn't want you to have to wait for that bus. Besides, it *was* on the way home once we got to the restaurant."

"You were so sweet. I was such an innocent young thing back then."

His naked lover dropped the towel to the floor and snorted as he sat on the bed. "Well, that didn't last long. I can't believe your roommate didn't catch us even once that first year."

"He was busy banging a girl from his art history class. I'm glad he moved out spring quarter to pledge a frat, though he *was* nice to look at when he came back from the showers." Bryant took off his black bow tie and unbuttoned his tux shirt. Desire flooded him as he stared at his lover's lean body. His cock pushed against the fabric of his slacks.

Alan watched him take off his shirt. "Geez, how is it possible you're just as beautiful now as you were twenty years ago?"

Bryant turned away from him, warmth spreading across his

face. Alan still knew all the right things to say. He opened the clasp on his slacks and bent over, pushing them and his underwear down.

"Damn, honey, just like when you dropped your keys the day I asked you to move in."

He tried to stifle his laugh. "I wasn't dropping my drawers then."

"Your ass still looked fine framed in your work slacks. I hope you're coming to bed with me soon." Alan gasped as Bryant turned to face him. "You're hard as a rock."

Bryant smiled, love and lust coursing through his body, battling for dominance. "You've always done this to me, but tonight I'm extra hard for you." He raked his gaze over Alan's stretched-out form. Age had started to show: a few more lines on his face and graying chest hair. After all, he was fifteen years older. Even younger men didn't turn him on like Alan did. His solid muscular legs sent Bryant's heart racing at each glance, still strong though they'd stopped dancing years before.

Bryant joined his lover on the bed, putting his head on Alan's chest. Black and white hair tickled his face and he smiled as he brushed it away from his nose. "I've been waiting all day for this."

Alan's fingers traced their way up Bryant's back. "Me, too. The party was great, but this is the best part."

Bryant basked in the warmth and the light thumping in Alan's chest. "I love listening to your heartbeat." He lifted his head and pressed his lips into Alan's neck, nipping and licking his way over his chin. He climbed on top of his lover and kissed him deeply. Alan's hands traveled up Bryant's stomach and ribs, leaving goose bumps in their wake as he wrapped his arms around his shivering younger lover's torso and pulled him into an embrace as their tongues dueled. Every point of contact with

Alan exploded in a shower of sparks just under the surface of Bryant's skin.

Alan rolled them over and maneuvered a pillow under Bryant's head. He kissed his way down his chest and stomach, sending jolts of lustful heat into Bryant. When he reached Bryant's cock, he pressed his lips around the base and on the inside of his thigh, bringing his tongue over his balls. He pulled the hardness away from Bryant's body and looked into his eyes. "I love you."

Bryant threw his head back into the pillow as a loud groan escaped his lips. He clutched the sheets as Alan sucked his cock to the root. His fingers grasped the sheets and he writhed as his senses overloaded in pleasure. The pressure increased, and Bryant's hips pumped into Alan's mouth. Tingling started in his balls, causing him to moan even louder.

Alan backed off panting. "I love how you taste, baby."

Gasping for breath, Bryant pulled Alan up to kiss him again. Alan pressed his cock against Bryant's rock-hard shaft and ground his hips. Bryant met his lover's thrusts as his fingers clawed at Alan's back, nearing his release. "Oh, babe, I'm gonna shoot."

Alan pushed off of him and flopped onto his back. "There's only one place I want that load right now, and it's not across my stomach." He spread his legs and pulled his knees up to his chest.

Bryant's desire for the man he loved burned white hot. He jumped between Alan's legs and darted his tongue into Alan's exposed hole.

"Oh yeah, that's hot." Alan hooked his arms under his knees. "Fuck, eat me out. Get me ready for that thick monster."

Digging deeper, Bryant rimmed his lover into a moaning and whimpering mass of man. He slid his body up and pushed his shoulders against the back of Alan's knees. Alan's hands went to Bryant's ass and clamped on, pulling him closer.

"Are you ready for me?"

Alan positioned him so that Bryant's cock lined up for entry. "Take me."

"Want some lube?"

Alan shook his head. "Put some spit on it and ease it in."

Bryant covered his head and shaft in saliva, then pushed into his lover. "Oh, baby, you feel so good."

Alan winced. "Let me get used to you, and then pound the hell out of me."

Bryant slid farther in as Alan relaxed and paused when he was buried to the hilt. They stayed like that for a few moments, Bryant's dick pulsing from the warmth and tightness around it. Alan squeezed and pushed his ass against Bryant's cock. "I'm ready. Make love to me the way you know I like."

"Your wish is my command." He backed out a little bit, then rammed home. He pounded his moaning lover deep into the soft mattress, kissing him as he fucked him hard. Lustful fire burned bright inside of Bryant. In the twenty years that he'd known and loved Alan, he had never experienced this level of desire. They were joined in so many ways now, but he yearned to fill him with his seed and make their joining that day complete.

Alan groaned out his desire, pitch increasing with each of Bryant's thrusts. "Yeah, baby, yeah. Take me. Love me. I'm yours."

His speed increasing, Bryant angled his cock to provide Alan the most pleasure. Alan moaned and gasped with each thrust. He dug his toes into the sheets and plowed deep.

"Oh fuck, I'm gonna shoot." Alan's back arched, his muscular legs pushing down hard onto Bryant's shoulders. His load blasted against his chest and hit Bryant's chin.

Bryant wiped it off with his arm and kept up his rhythm. The squeezing from Alan's orgasm pulled him over the edge. "Yeah, I'm there, too. Ready to fill you." His eyes rolled before he closed his lids and screamed out his release.

Alan's lips found his, and their lips pressed together as Bryant shook. The aftermath of his explosion and the intense emotions flooding through him drained his energy. Alan pulled him to his chest as Bryant's cock slid out of him. He pressed his heaving body against his lover.

Bryant's breathing returned to normal after a few minutes. He ran his hand over Alan's chest. "You're a mess."

"Are you complaining?"

Bryant smiled. "Not in the slightest." He moved to Alan's side. "I love you, Alan Hansen."

Alan wrapped his arm around Bryant's torso. "I love you, too. Marrying you was the best move I've ever made."

"Nah." Bryant snuggled into his side. "Dropping your drawers when I opened the door and then taking me home was by far your best move."

WEDDING
DAY JITTERS

Rob Rosen

I woke up in a cold sweat, eyes stinging, head pounding. "I think I'm dying," I lamented, wiping the torrent off my forehead and groaning as I did so.

John, my partner, snorted. "No, Peter; just getting married. Now go back to sleep."

"But it's already light outside."

The snort was repeated. "That's the moon, dearest."

"Oh."

"Yeah, oh." He rolled toward me and took my hand in his before replacing the snort with a heavy sigh. "Why so nervous, anyway? Everything's been taken care of."

A list began rolling in my head before spewing forth from between my parched lips. "What if it rains? What if no one shows? What if everyone shows? Did I put the stamps on all the invitations or did I miss some? Did I pay the caterer, the minister, the rental hall, the florist? Does my tux fit? Do I look fat in it?"

He squeezed my hand. "Please stop, Peter. Now *I'm* nervous."

"See."

He huffed while I puffed, both of us staring up at the ceiling, my heart beating out a mad samba in my chest. "So much for sleeping." He looked over my shoulder at the alarm clock on the nightstand. "Only eight more hours to go."

The pit in my stomach ripened into an overgrown melon. "Plus six minutes." I gulped. "Make that five." The gulp repeated. "And counting."

He slapped the bed and then quickly sprung up. "Okay, enough of this. Put your shorts on; we're going for a jog."

I stared at him incredulously. "At this hour?"

He tilted his head my way. "Any better ideas? Besides, it always relaxes you."

"So does a Xanax, a margarita and a *Golden Girls* marathon. Not necessarily in the order." I reconsidered. "Okay, exactly in that order."

He tossed me my shorts. "No Xanax, the bars are all closed, nothing on TV worth watching. Or, in two more hours, we can either watch Sunday morning prayer services, *Sesame Street*, or perhaps expand our cable service. Take your pick."

I grabbed for the shorts and lumbered out of bed, grumbling all the while. "Really, no Xanax?"

He shrugged. "Gave the last one to your mom."

I couldn't help but chuckle. "Now you know where I get my neuroses from."

"Trust me," he retorted, "I know. And I'm marrying you just the same."

I spanked his ass and ran around him before scooting out the bedroom door. "Sucker," I yelled over my shoulder. He was already galloping behind me as I reached the front door, where I quickly slipped on my sneakers. I raced outside, a warm summer breeze washing over my exposed chest and bare knees. John was jogging next to me a moment later as we made our way up the driveway and into the night—well, night*ish*, soon to be morning*esque.*

"Funny," he said as we rounded the corner, a dog barking at us from behind a fence.

"What, that we're out jogging or that in just under eight hours we'll be getting married?" My gulp watered the melon in my gut, a veritable orchard sprouting in its place.

"No," he replied, "that we're jogging on the day we're getting married, and that's—"

"How we met!" I shouted, finishing his train of thought. "Funny."

"I already said that."

I nodded my head. "Great minds think alike."

Which is why we both knew where to head from there, our paces picking up, legs pounding the pavement, a fresh line of sweat trickling down my chest as we tore through our neighborhood to the park barely a mile away. In we raced, laughing as he tried to beat me to the entrance and I tried to beat him. In the end, it was a tie. Same thing as the beginning, nine years earlier almost to the day. On that fateful afternoon, I was running to the water fountain, while he was running to it from the opposite direction. He spotted me, I spotted him, a race ensued. Like I said, we tied—in that we both reached the fountain at the same time, our heads colliding in a thunderous crash, stars swimming before my eyes.

"Which reminds me. Did you invite Doctor Marsh?"

He nodded as he sipped from the spigot. "He's bringing his medical bag. Just in case."

I pushed John over a couple of inches and craned my neck

down, the cool water instantly gliding down my hot throat. "Smart."

I stood. He stood. He grinned as he placed his fingertips on my forehead, admiring the good doctor's handiwork. I aped the gesture on his forehead. "Great minds scar alike, too."

His fingers lingered, tracing their way down my cheek, my neck, my clavicle. They landed on a breeze-stiffened nipple. I stared down at his midsection. Apparently, my nipple wasn't the only thing stiffened.

"Um, what are you doing?"

He also stared down, moving his hips from side to side so that his burgeoning stiffy swung within his meager shorts. "Taking your mind off of, um, *things*."

I watched as he then grabbed said shorts from the bottom, scrunched up the cotton trim, and released the beast within. "Well, that's one way to do it," I commented as I continued staring. It hung in midair, bathed in a silver glow, balls swaying a mere second later.

Again he swung his prized prick, a breeze seemingly rising in its ample wake. "It looks lonely."

I dropped my shorts to the ground and kicked them off, leaving me in nothing but my sneakers and an erection that could crack open a safe—if, in fact, you felt like wasting a perfectly good erection that way. "Well, I must say, you get an A for effort, John." I gave it a tug and a squeeze. "A-plus."

He sunk to his knees. "Amen."

My handsome husband-to-be downed my chubby in one fell swoop, a gagging tear streaming down his scruffy cheek as he sucked me off and yanked on my nuts. Another breeze wafted over us, goose bumps riding down my arms as I pinched my nipples and watched his steady progress. "Can two play this game?" I eventually thought to ask.

My swollen, moonlit prick popped out of his mouth, spit flinging off the tip and down his chin. "I thought two were." He wiped the saliva away and stood up, his own shorts now kicked off, leaving us both like the trees that surrounded us: erect and wooden. "Follow me, fiancé."

"Anywhere, fiancé."

Hand in hand, shorts gripped in our free mitts, like Adam and Steve, we made our way through Eden (better known as City Park West) and headed for the grassy knoll in the rear— the park's rear, not mine, which was neither grassy nor knolly, though it was indeed in John's face barely a minute later. He was flat on his back, I was straddling him, my mouth down (way down) on his dick, my rear, as mentioned, pressed up tightly to his mouth. It was a perfect seventy: sixty-nine plus a bonus point for location, which, as they say, is everything.

His crotch smelled of sweat and musk, plus a little zesty fertilizer thrown in for good measure. His cock filled my mouth as it glided down my throat, his heavy, hairy balls rolling between my dexterous fingers all the while. He bucked into me, while I pushed into him, until it was impossible to tell where he ended and I began. Ironically, that was our life in a nutshell as well.

While I sucked and slobbered and licked and tugged, he ate my ass out with gusto, his tongue swirling inside of me as he stroked my cock between my splayed thighs. White-hot volts of adrenaline shot down my spine as the sky above began to turn from murky black to a deep, dark blue. And then, to up the ante, and knowing me all too well, he slid a spit-slick digit deep inside my hole and gave it a swirl, causing my cock to throb.

"Mmm," I moaned, my back arching as a second finger joined the fray.

Never one to be outdone, and while I continued sucking gleefully away, I let my wedding-ring finger (still, for the time being, unadorned) worm its way inside his silky hole. And then two of us were moaning up a storm, a flock of pigeons suddenly taking wing from somewhere nearby, apparently disturbed out of their morning slumber. Them and me both, I figured.

"Three's my lucky number," I reminded him, very nearly breathless at his ministrations.

He chuckled, his fingering duo quickly a pistoning trio. "I know, my dear. I know. And mine is—"

"Four!" And, wouldn't you know it, four wet fingers were now pummeling his ultra-tight tush. "I know, my dear. I know." Because, yes, there's something to be said for so intimately knowing your partner, as John and I obviously did.

Which is why his next request didn't surprise me all that much. Excite, sure, but surprise, nuh-uh. "You ever fuck anyone in a sling before, Peter?" he panted, most of my hand buried so far up his ass that it was a wonder I wasn't waving from inside his mouth at the time.

I stopped pumping and turned my head to the side. "A sling, John? Trust me, there isn't one hidden up here."

He spanked my ass, and I moaned in rapturous delight. "How about the next best thing?"

I scrunched my face in thought—either that or because his triple digits were snugly pressing up to my ever-hardening prostate. "The next best thing to a sling out in the middle of a park in the middle of, well, whatever time it is?" Suddenly, a proverbial lightbulb pulsed above my not-so-proverbial noggin. "You dirty boy."

He chuckled and retracted his hand from inside my hole. "Which is why you love me."

I retracted my hand from his hole. "Among the many other reasons."

He helped me up off the grass and once again held my hand.

Off we walked to the playground at the side of the knoll, rigid cocks swaying all the while as we looked into the near darkness for signs of any intruders, apart from us and the wayward pigeons. Thankfully, we were the only naked, horny, hard men to be found. Go figure. Guess they were all at home, waiting for *Sesame Street* to start.

In any case, I quickly spotted the *sling* in question. That is to say, the swing, long meant for children to squeal while riding on, would now be making my husband-to-be squeal instead. Yippy for public-funded city parks.

"Dirty boy," I quipped as we entered the playground.

"You already said that."

"Bears repeating." I glanced into his sparkling eyes of blue and grinned. "And since you're already, um, *bare...*"

He hopped on the swing. "*Whee*," he squealed, not too surprisingly, as he gave a push with his legs, which were quickly dangling as well as spread wide. "Now start that promised repeating."

I stood in front of the apparatus and stopped his to and fro. His legs went up higher and wider, hole winking out my way. I crouched down, my cock in my left hand, mouth to his chute, tongue licking and lapping, sucking and biting, all while he stroked himself and moaned with abandon, his balls bouncing on the bridge of my nose.

"You smell grassy," I mumbled, in between hearty slurps.

"Assy?" he purred, hand rapid-firing on his pole, eyes in a squint.

I shrugged. "That too." I slid a slicked finger inside of him, in and up and back. His purr turned to a rumbling groan, thundering when two fingers joined the first, louder still when they became a pumping quartet. And then he set the swing to swinging, yet again. Out popped my fingers, *whoosh* went his ass; *whoosh* it went in reverse, in went my fingers. Steps one through four were repeated again and again and again, all while he stroked and I stroked and our balls slowly did their inevitable rises upward.

On the last *whoosh* and *whee*, he stopped the swing by wrapping his feet around my sweat-soaked back, my fingers once again deeply entrenched up his ass. He threw his head back and howled his way into the day. The *whoosh* and the *whee* were then joined by a *plop, plop, plop* as his come flew up and then rained down, splashing on his wildly expanding and contracting belly.

"*Fuuuck,*" he exhaled, the pungently pleasing aroma of come wafting languidly up my nostrils.

"Just did," I rasped, hopping up as I gave my cock one final tug, the come spewing up and out before joining the puddle of spunk on his hairy abs.

He lowered his sneakered feet to the ground, the pool of jizz sliding down before dripping off. I smiled at him as I fought to catch my breath, then leaned in for a deep soulful kiss, the kind that made my very soul pulse—and my cock; take your pick.

Still drenched, not to mention awfully sticky, we found our shorts, slid them back on and prepared for the jog back. "Look!" John suddenly shouted, index finger pointed to the sky.

My eyes followed his digit's trajectory. "Nice," I exhaled, staring at the blue sky as it turned a stunning purple, pink already at the periphery, a promise of blistering orange at the horizon.

Hand in hand we again made our way to the grassy knoll. We lay down beside each other and watched as the morning yawned its way into existence, the colors morphing, growing as bright as the future that lay ahead.

Though, of course, when two sex-drained and newly relaxed

men, who've barely slept a wink, lie on the cool grass as the sun begins to warm them with its first rays of the day, well, it's sort of easy to figure out what happened next.

In other words, when I awoke, *Sesame Street* was long over and done with, and the sky was no longer pink and orange. Instead, it was a cool, crisp blue, not a cloud to be seen.

"John," I grunted, poking his side. "Wake up."

He twitched and covered his face with his hand. "Are we married yet?"

I hopped up and wiped the grass off my shorts. "Not even close." I reached my hand down to help him up. "Hurry up, John!"

I didn't have a watch on, and he didn't have a watch on—heck, we were barely dressed as it was—but I knew it was late. Though lord only knew how much of the eight hours and five minutes (and counting) we had left.

Needless to say, we ran faster than we'd ever run before, covering that mile in what seemed like mere seconds before rushing inside the house and up the stairs to the bedroom. I looked at John and he looked at me. "Forty-three minutes!" we both shouted in unison. And counting. "Fuck!" And, no, that wasn't the good kind of "fuck" this time.

So off the sneakers came, the shorts were shucked and into the shower we ran, me soaping him up, him lathering me, both of us shampooing ourselves. We were car wash meets whirling dervish in the blink of eye. Then I shaved while he brushed his teeth and he shaved while I brushed mine. I blow-dried while he towel-dried, deodorized while he talcumed.

Again we looked at each other, then at the bedroom clock. "Sixteen minutes!" Last time: and counting. Mainly because that was the last time we had time to look. Or dared to.

On went the dress shirts, the socks and underwear, the

slacks, the belts, the vests, the jackets and the bow ties, and all in a dazzling blue—to match his eyes, which would make the sky outside jealous. And, just as we put the finishing touches on all of that: hair gel, cufflinks, a spritz of Polo Blue, we heard it.

"Limo's here!" he shouted the obvious.

I looked at him, he looked at me and we both smiled, a flush of warmth suddenly spreading through me. "You look very handsome, fiancé," I told him.

"Ditto, fiancé."

And then, once again, we tore downstairs, our rental shoes clomping loudly as we raced outside, a beautiful late morning breeze hitting our faces. The limo driver was waiting by the passenger door, which he opened just before we climbed inside.

My mother was already waiting inside the limo for us, John's mother right beside her. The dads were at the hall, arranging the finishing touches. I plopped down, John plopped next to me and we both smiled at the women sitting across from us.

"You look relaxed," said my mom. "Good night's sleep?"

I laughed until my side hurt, John coughing all the while. "The best, Ma," I eventually replied. "You look relaxed as well."

"Xanax," she replied, a hazy yet joyous expression blanketing her face.

John looked at his mother. "What's your excuse?"

She pointed at my mother. "We went halfsies." And then they handed us each a frosty margarita.

Ah, family!

Ten minutes later, we were pulling up to the hall, flowers festooning the entryway, a GOOD LUCK, JOHN & PETER sign hanging above the door. I had a feeling that luck was something we already had plenty of. And love, of course.

I was no longer worried or stressed or nervous (or horny)—
thanks to my soon-to-be husband—as we entered the hall, our
friends and family all turning, all clapping and smiling. And,
no, it never rained that day; everyone showed up; I had, it
appeared, put stamps on all the invitations; I had, it seemed,
paid the caterer, the minister, the rental hall and the florist; and,
yes, my tux fit beautifully, and, no, I didn't look fat in it at all. In
fact, if I looked half as stunning as John, we were probably the
two most spectacularly handsome (and happy) grooms getting
married anywhere that day.

A-plus and amen yet again.

Whee!

ABOUT THE AUTHORS

KRISTA ANDERSON, writing as Krista Merlc, has been a massage therapist, a preschool teacher and a magazine writer. When she's not working at her local library, she writes erotica and dark fantasy. She lives in Columbia, SC but misses her Jersey home.

BRENT ARCHER started writing in 2011, and had his first short story, "Dear Bryan," published in 2012 by Ravenous Romance. He had several short stories published in 2014 by Cleis Press. When not writing, he enjoys acting, gardening and traveling to research new stories.

KITTEN BOHEME, (kittenboheme.com) besides being an avid reader and writer of erotica, is also a published playwright. When not writing, she pursues her interests in the European aristocracy and the occult. She lives a nomadic lifestyle with Franklin, her cat, and an angry goldfish, Sir Swimsalot.

MICHAEL BRACKEN is the author of several books and more than one thousand short stories, including erotic fiction published in *Best Gay Erotica 2013, Best Gay Romance 2010* and *2013, Model Men, Steam Bath, Ultimate Gay Erotica 2006* and many other anthologies and magazines. He lives and writes in Texas.

HEIDI CHAMPA has been published in numerous anthologies including *College Boys, Big Man on Campus, Skater Boys* and *Steam Bath.* More stories can be found at Dreamspinner Press, Amber Allure and Torquere Press. Find more online at heidichampa.blogspot.com.

JAMESON DASH lives and writes in the Pacific Northwest, where you learn to love the rain.

KIWI ROXANNE DUNN has published the erotic short stories "Hunger Pains" and "Birthday Presents" with Dreamspinner Press.

D. K. JERNIGAN (jerniganwrites@gmail.com) loves men who love men, hard cider and long walks on the beach. He lives in California with the most amazing husband in the world and a devoted German Shepherd, and has been published in *Spellbinding: Tales from the Magic University* from Ravenous Romance.

RHIDIAN BRENIG JONES has herded sheep in New Zealand, taught English in Poland and run a bar on the Costa del Sol. Now settled back home in Wales, he leads an adult literacy program and writes whenever he can snatch a spare hour or two. He lives with his husband, Michael, and two arthritic old Labradors.

JUSTIN JOSH has worked as a carpet cleaner, fast-food cook, data-entry clerk, teacher, writer, payroll specialist, actor and bookkeeper. A lifelong fan of gay male erotica, he recently began writing his own stories. This is his first sale. He currently resides in Reseda, California.

OLEANDER PLUME (oleanderplume.blogspot.com) believes everyone has the right to create her own happily ever after, and that love in all its forms is a beautiful thing. She also writes erotica sometimes.

P. L. RIPLEY is a born storyteller, weaving worlds since he could first express what he saw in his head. Fascinated with human sexuality, erotic fiction is a natural place for him to explore the connection between sexual excitement and our emotional responses to it. He lives near Bangor, Maine, with his partner.

ROB ROSEN (therobrosen.com), award-winning author of the novels *Sparkle: The Queerest Book You'll Ever Love*, *Divas Las Vegas*, *Hot Lava*, *Southern Fried*, *Queerwolf* and *Vamp*, and editor of the anthologies *Lust in Time* and *Men of the Manor*, has had short stories featured in more than 180 anthologies.

Unbeknownst to her dissertation committee, **T. R. VERTEN** was really a spy in the house of academia. She is the author of the gay erotic novella *Confessions of a Rentboy*, now republished by Burning Book Press. You can find her on Twitter, @trepverten where she talks about hot boys, her cats and what's for dinner.

LOGAN ZACHARY (loganzacharydicklit.com) is the author of *Calendar Boys* and *Big Bad Wolf*, an erotic werewolf mystery.

His stories can also be found in: *Going Down, Best Bondage Stories of 2013, Tricks of the Trade, Big Men on Campus, Beach Bums, Sexy Sailors* and *The Spy Who Laid Me.*

ABOUT
THE EDITOR

NEIL PLAKCY is the author of more than twenty novels and collections of short stories, as well as the editor of many anthologies for Cleis Press. He began his erotic writing career with a story for *Honcho* magazine called "The Cop Who Caught Me," and he's been writing about cops and sex ever since, most recently with seven novels in the Mahu mystery series. He lives in South Florida, and his website is mahubooks.com.

The Best in Gay Romance

Best Gay Romance 2014
Edited by Timothy Lambert and R. D. Cochrane

The best part of romance is what might happen next...that pivotal moment where we stop and realize, *This is wonderful.* But most of all, love—whether new or lifelong—creates endless possibilities. *Best Gay Romance 2014* reminds us all of how love changes us for the better.
ISBN 978-1-62778-011-7 $15.95

The Handsome Prince
Gay Erotic Romance
Edited by Neil Plakcy

In this one and only gay erotic fairy tale anthology, your prince will come—and come again!
ISBN 978-1-57344-659-4 $14.95

Afternoon Pleasures
Erotica for Gay Couples
Edited by Shane Allison

Filled with romance, passion and lots of lust, *Afternoon Pleasures* is irresistibly erotic yet celebrates the coming together of souls as well as bodies.
ISBN 978-1-57344-658-7 $14.95

Fool for Love
New Gay Fiction
Edited by Timothy Lambert and R. D. Cochrane

For anyone who believes that love has left the building, here is an exhilarating collection of new gay fiction designed to reignite your belief in the power of romance.
ISBN 978-1-57344-339-5 $14.95

Boy Crazy
Coming Out Erotica
Edited by Richard Labonté

Editor Richard Labonté's unique collection of coming-out tales celebrates first-time lust, first-time falling into bed, and first discovery of love.
ISBN 978-1-57344-351-7 $14.95

Get Under the Covers
with These Hunks

Men on the Make

Wild Boys
Gay Erotic Fiction
Edited by Richard Labonté

Take a walk on the wild side with these fierce tales of rough trade. Defy the rules and succumb to the charms of hustlers, jocks, kinky tricks, smart-asses, con men, straight guys and gutter punks who give as good as they get.
ISBN 978-1-57344-824-6 $15.95

Sexy Sailors
Gay Erotic Stories
Edited by Neil Plakcy

Award-winning editor Neil Plakcy has collected bold stories of naughty, nautical hunks and wild, stormy sex that are sure to blow your imagination.
ISBN 978-1-57344-822-2 $15.95

Hot Daddies
Gay Erotic Fiction
Edited by Richard Labonté

From burly bears and hunky father figures to dominant leathermen, *Hot Daddies* captures the erotic dynamic between younger and older men: intense connections, consensual submission, and the toughest and tenderest of teaching and learning.
ISBN 978-1-57344-712-6 $14.95

Straight Guys
Gay Erotic Fantasies
Edited by Shane Allison

Gaybie Award-winner Shane Allison shares true and we-wish-they-were-true stories in his bold collection. From a husband on the down low to a muscle-bound footballer, and from a special operations airman to a redneck daddy, these men will sweep you off your feet.
ISBN 978-1-57344-816-1 $15.95

Cruising
Gay Erotic Stories
Edited by Shane Allison

Homemade glory holes in a stall wall, steamy shower trysts, truck stop rendezvous...according to Shane Allison, "There's nothing that gets the adrenaline flowing and the muscle throbbing like public sex."
ISBN 978-1-57344-786-7 $14.95

Rousing, Arousing
Adventures with Hot Hunks

Ordering is easy! Call us toll free or fax us to place your MC/VISA order.
You can also mail the order form below with payment to:
Cleis Press, 2246 Sixth St., Berkeley, CA 94710.

ORDER FORM

QTY	TITLE	PRICE

SUBTOTAL _____

SHIPPING _____

SALES TAX _____

TOTAL _____

Add $3.95 postage/handling for the first book ordered and $1.00 for each additional
book. Outside North America, please contact us for shipping rates. California residents
add 9% sales tax. Payment in U.S. dollars only.

* Free book of equal or lesser value. Shipping and applicable sales tax extra.

Cleis Press • Phone: (800) 780-2279 • Fax: (510) 845-8001
orders@cleispress.com • www.cleispress.com
You'll find more great books on our website

Follow us on Twitter @cleispress • Friend/fan us on Facebook